# THE MASK WEARER

# Amos Daragon

## THE MASK WEARER

*Translated from the French by Y. Maudet*

BRYAN PERRO

BLUEFIRE

Visit us on the Web! www.randomhouse.com/kids
Educators and librarians, for a variety of teaching tools, visit us at
www.randomhouse.com/teachers

The Library of Congress has cataloged the hardcover edition of this work as follows:
Perro, Bryan.
[Porteur de masques. English]
The mask wearer / Bryan Perro ; translated from the French by Y. Maudet. — 1st U.S. ed.
p. cm. — (Amos Daragon)
Summary: To defeat the forces of evil which threaten his world, young Amos Daragon, aided by mythical animal friends, sets out on a journey to find four masks that harness the forces of nature and sixteen powerful stones that give the masks their magic.
ISBN 978-0-385-73903-0 (hc : alk. paper) — ISBN 978-0-385-90766-8 (glb : alk. paper) —
ISBN 978-0-375-89693-4 (ebook)
[1. Fantasy. 2. Adventure and adventurers—Fiction. 3. Prophecies—Fiction.
4. Good and evil—Fiction.] I. Maudet, Y. II. Title.
PZ7.P4342Mas 2011
[Fic]—dc22
2010023725

ISBN 978-0-375-85976-2 (pbk.)

RL: 5.0

Printed in the United States of America
10 9 8 7 6 5 4 3 2 1
First Bluefire Edition 2012

# Contents

# *PROLOGUE*

Among the world's most ancient legends exists the story of masks endowed with great power. These masks—priceless and known to bear the sacred magic of the elements—were given to a few human beings who possessed tremendous courage and spirit. There were four masks: one each for earth, air, fire, and water, as well as sixteen stones from which the masks drew their extraordinary strength. In the eternal fight between good and evil, between day and night, between the gods of the positive and negative worlds, the task of these chosen humans was to restore the balance between these forces.

Amos Daragon, son of Urban and Frilla Daragon, was one of those selected to accomplish this mission. From the day of his birth, his destiny was foretold by the Lady in White, who wrote it down in gold letters in the great history of heroes. As supreme goddess of the world, she was patiently waiting for the day Amos would realize his potential.

—1—

# THE BAY OF CAVERNS

The realm of Omain was a magnificent place. A dark-stoned castle overlooked a small city with tidy streets. High above, mountains whose tops were covered in perpetual snow encircled the kingdom. From these snowy tops, a wide and winding river cascaded down the slopes and ran directly to the center of town in the valley.

There was also a small fishing seaport swarming with small and brightly colored boats. When the hush of nighttime fell over the fish market, the citizens were lulled to sleep by the sound of the ocean waves. Every morning, dozens of fishermen followed the river, raising the triangular sails of their wooden boats and casting their nets and fishing lines into the cove.

The streets of Omain were unpaved. One traveled them either on foot or riding a donkey. Every inhabitant was poor, with the exception of Lord Edonf, who lived in the castle. He was the ruler of this little paradise and demanded that each family pay huge taxes for the upkeep of the kingdom. Each month, on the full moon, the lord's personal guard came down to collect the tax money.

If a citizen was unable to pay, he was immediately thrown into an iron cage and exposed to gaping onlookers in the center of the market. Deprived of food and water, suffering from the cold, or from the heat and mosquitoes, the wretched person often stayed caged for days, even weeks. The town dwellers knew that being placed in the cage was usually a death sentence for the prisoner. So everyone tried to scrupulously pay Lord Edonf his dues.

Edonf was as fat as a whale. And with eyes that popped out of their sockets, a large mouth, and oily skin covered with pimples, he looked exactly like one of the huge sea toads that invaded the fishing village once a year in the spring. In addition to being frighteningly ugly, Edonf was said to have a brain the size of a tadpole's. By the hearths in all the houses, the elders told the children stories about the incredible stupidity of their ruler. Of course, these tales were embellished over time, taking on new life depending on the talent of the teller, but they never failed to delight both young and old.

So it was that everyone in Omain knew the story of Yack the Troubadour, who had passed through town to entertain the villagers with his company of buffoons. He had pretended to be a famous doctor, and for nearly a month, Lord Edonf followed his advice. Yack made Edonf swallow lamb droppings coated in sugar as a cure for forgetfulness. Ever since, it was said that Edonf had totally recovered his memory and would never forget the fake doctor—or the taste of lamb droppings. The elders of Omain were now in the habit of telling their children that if they ever forgot to obey their parents, they too would get a taste of Yack's medicine. Once they heard this tale, every child always had an excellent memory.

Ψ

Amos Daragon was born in Omain. His father and mother were both craftspeople and had traveled for years looking for the ideal spot to settle down. When they discovered the lush land of Omain, they decided to stay, convinced that they would remain there until the end of their days.

But this honest couple made a serious mistake when they built a little cottage on the edge of the forest, not far from town, on land belonging to Lord Edonf. When Edonf heard the news, he sent his guards to pay them a visit, and ordered that they be caged and their house burned. In exchange for their lives and for the trees they had felled to build their humble house, Urban Daragon suggested that Lord Edonf allow him to work for his lordship without pay to reimburse his debt. Edonf agreed. Twelve years had gone by since that sad day, and Amos's father was still paying by the sweat of his brow for his past mistake.

After so much time toiling on behalf of Lord Edonf, Urban was a pitiful sight. He had lost a great deal of weight and was wasting away. Edonf treated him like a slave, always demanding more of him. The last few years had been particularly difficult for Urban, as his master had started to cudgel him to make him work faster. The ruler of Omain took pleasure in beating Urban, who had no choice but to endure Edonf's wrath. Every day Amos's father came back home humiliated, his limbs sore. Since he didn't have enough money to flee the realm, or enough strength to confront Edonf and break away from him, he left his home defeated every morning and returned bloodied every night.

The Daragon family was the poorest in the village, and their cottage was the smallest of all. Its walls were made of roughly hewed tree trunks laid on top of each other. To retain the warmth of the hearth, Urban Daragon had filled all the holes with hay and peat moss to make them airtight. The straw roof was fully waterproof, and the big stone chimney, huge compared to the size of the house, seemed to be the only sturdy part of the dwelling. A small flower garden, mostly shaded because of the big trees surrounding it, and a minuscule building vaguely resembling a barn completed the picture.

Inside the cottage, a wooden table, three chairs, and bunk beds were the only furniture. The chimney occupied almost all the surface of the east wall. A cooking pot was always hanging on the hook above the fire. Living here meant a constant battle against heat and cold, against hunger and poverty.

Since childhood, Amos had acquired many skills. He hunted pheasant and hare in the forest, fished in the river with an improvised fishing rod, and collected shellfish on the ocean shores. Thanks to him, the family managed to survive, even if on some days there wasn't much on the table.

Over the years, Amos had perfected an almost foolproof way of catching edible birds. He used a long branch shaped like a Y, along which he slid a cord with a slipknot at the end.

When he spotted a partridge, he stayed a good distance from his prey, only slowly moving the forked end of the branch toward the animal. Noiselessly, Amos would slip the knot around the bird's neck and suddenly pull on the cord. In this manner, he often brought home the family dinner.

Amos learned to listen to nature, to blend in among the ferns, and to walk noiselessly in the woods. By the time he was twelve years old, he was familiar with the different types of trees and their fruits and nuts, knew the best spots for finding wild berries, and could track all the animals of the forest. Sometimes, during the cold season, he unearthed truffles, mushrooms that grow underground, at the base of oak trees. The forest held no secrets from him.

But Amos was deeply unhappy. Every day, he saw his father suffering and his mother declining in spirit. Always short of money, his parents often argued. They had sunk into a daily misery that they couldn't get out of. When they were younger, Urban's and Frilla's eyes had sparkled, and they were always making travel plans, happy to be carefree. Now their eyes showed only sadness and exhaustion, and they never went anywhere. Every night, Amos dreamed of saving his parents and giving them a better life. He also dreamed of having a mentor who would explain the world to him; his parents were too poor to send him to school, and he longed for someone to answer his questions and advise him as to what to read. Every night, Amos Daragon went to sleep hoping that tomorrow would bring him a better life.

ψ

One beautiful summer morning, Amos went down to the beach to gather some mussels and dislodge a few crabs. He followed his usual path without much success. The little he had gathered sat at the bottom of one of his two wooden buckets; it wouldn't be enough to feed three people.

*Well!* he thought. *That's all I'm going to find here. But it's still early and the sun is shining, so I'll go and see what I can find on another beach.*

Amos was all set to go to an unfamiliar spot when he remembered the bay of caverns. It was a good ways off, but he had gone there a few times and knew that if he hurried now, and quickened his pace on his way back, he would be home before the end of the afternoon, as he had promised his father.

The bay of caverns was a place where the ebb and flow of the tides had eroded and hollowed the stones to form grottoes, ponds, and impressive sculptures. Amos had stumbled upon the spot, where he always managed to gather a large quantity of crabs and mussels. But the great distance kept him from going there regularly. With a large bucket filled to the rim in each hand, the way back home was never easy.

After a two-hour walk, Amos finally reached the bay of caverns. Exhausted, he sat on the beach pebbles and contemplated the low tide and the immense sculptures cut by the ocean that presided over the bay like petrified giants. Everywhere on the cliff, Amos could see the gaping holes created by thousands of years of tides, waves, and storms. The cool wind from the open sea caressed his tanned skin, and the high sun burned his nose.

"Now, Amos, let's get started!" he told himself.

He quickly filled his two buckets with crabs. On the beach, dozens more had been overtaken by low tide and were trying to get back to the salty water. As Amos passed by the entrance of a grotto that was larger and higher than the others, he spotted a big black crow, dead on the shore. Amos raised his eyes toward the sky and saw at least twenty more flying in circles above the cliff.

*That's the way these birds fly when another animal is dying*, he thought. *They'll feed on the corpse. Maybe it's a big fish or a stranded whale. This dead crow wasn't lucky. He probably broke his neck on the rock.*

As he carefully looked around for a helpless animal, Amos saw three more crows at the entrance of the grotto, but these were alive. Their eyes seemed riveted inside the cavern, as if they were trying to make sense of something in the belly of the rocky wall. Amos was approaching to find out what was going on when he heard a piercing scream. It came from the depths of the cavern; the frightening sound paralyzed the birds. They fell dead on the spot.

Amos himself was knocked down—as if hit by a strong blow—by the intensity of the scream. He lay curled up, his heart beating madly. His legs refused to move. He had never heard such a noise. The scream, which seemed both human and animal, had to have been shrieked by powerful vocal cords.

Then Amos heard a woman's voice, as soft as a melody, and he came out of his daze. It was as if a lyre, hidden deeply in the grotto, had begun to play.

"Don't be scared, young man. I am not an enemy," the voice said.

Amos raised his head and got back on his feet. He left his buckets where he had dropped them.

"I'm in the grotto. Come quickly; I am waiting for you. I won't hurt you. I screamed only to scare the birds away."

Gingerly, Amos approached the opening. The woman kept talking, her words sounding like a symphony of bells to Amos's ears.

"Have no fear. I am suspicious of the birds because they are nosy and rude," she said. "They spy, and they love to eat fish far too much to be trusted. When you see me, you'll understand what I mean. I'll tell you again that I intend no harm. Come quickly now; I don't have much time left."

Amos entered the grotto, feeling his way in the dark toward the voice. Suddenly, a soft blue light wrapped itself along the ground and uneven walls. Small puddles of water glistened. All the humidity of the cavern sparkled. It was magical. Each drop had its own shade of blue. This light filled the inside of the grotto, and Amos felt as if he were walking over a moving fluid.

"It's beautiful, isn't it?" the voice went on. "This is the light of my people. Everyone where I come from can create light out of salt water. Turn around—I'm here, very close by."

Amos turned. When he saw the creature, it took all his courage not to run away. In front of him, stretched out in a small puddle of water, was a mermaid. Her long hair was the pale color of the reflected light of sunset on the ocean. She wore an armor of shellfish on her strongly muscled torso, and

Amos thought he could see a cloth woven of algae between the armor and her skin. Her nails were long and sharp. A huge, wide fish tail ended her impressive body. Close to her was a weapon, an ivory trident, probably sculpted out of a narwhal tusk, decorated with light red coral.

"I can see fear in your eyes. Don't be afraid." The mermaid smiled. "I know that mermaids have a bad reputation among humans. Your legends say that we charm sailors to lure them to the bottom of the sea. These legends are not true. It's the merriens—sea creatures who resemble mermaids but who are repulsively ugly and brutal—who do this. The merriens use their voices to cast spells and ensnare seamen. Then they devour their victims, pilfer their cargos, and create storms to sink the ships that they use as dwellings deep in the ocean."

As she spoke, Amos noticed large cuts in her armor.

"Are you wounded?" he asked. "I'm sure I can help you. Let me go to the forest. I know some plants that could heal you."

"You're kind," the mermaid said. "Unfortunately, I am doomed to die soon. I was in a battle with merriens and my wounds are deep. At home, way down in the ocean, the war against these evil beings has raged on these last few days." She paused and held up an object. "What I want is for you to take this white stone and go to Gwenfadrille, who lives in the woods of Tarkasis. Tell her that her friend Crivannia, princess of the waters, is dead and that her kingdom has fallen into enemy hands. Tell her also that I've chosen you as the mask wearer. She'll understand and will act accordingly. Swear to me, on your life, that as soon as you can, you will leave to undertake this mission."

Without stopping to think, Amos agreed and swore on his life. He took the white stone from the mermaid and put it in one of his pockets.

"Go quickly now. Run and close your ears," the mermaid said. "A princess of the waters never passes away quietly. May the power of the elements guide you! And take the trident; it will be useful. Go!"

Amos grabbed the trident and hurried out of the grotto. As he covered his ears with his hands, he heard a mournful sound: a languid song, filled with sadness and pain, rang out over the whole bay and shook the ground beneath him. Stones began to fall here and there, and then, with a terrifying noise, the cavern where the mermaid lay dying collapsed violently. When it was over, a deep silence invaded the area.

Amos climbed up the cliff, the ivory trident slung over his shoulder, a bucket filled with crabs in each hand, and turned back to look at the collapsed grotto one last time. He knew that it was unlikely that he would ever see this bay of caverns again. As he gazed out, he saw hundreds of mermaids, their heads raised above the water, looking at the princess's tomb. And when he was already a good distance away, Amos heard a funeral song carried by the wind. A chorus of mermaids was paying a last tribute to Crivannia.

—2—

# LORD EDONF, THE STONE SOUP, AND THE HORSES

Amos arrived home in the late afternoon. To his great surprise, Lord Edonf was there, accompanied by two guards. In front of the cottage, Amos's parents, their heads lowered in submission, were listening to their ruler's abusive words. The fat man was red with anger and threatened to burn down the house. He was scolding the couple for having worked his land without permission and for having hunted shamelessly on his domain. What was more, he claimed that the family had a donkey that was his. The animal had apparently been stolen from within the walls of his castle.

On this point, Lord Edonf was right. During a short nighttime visit to the castle, Amos had kidnapped the animal to spare it from the bad treatment it endured. He then told his parents that he had found the donkey in the forest and that the animal had followed him to the house. Now Edonf was requesting a large amount of money to forget the wrongdoing, and Amos's parents, unable to pay, did not know what to say or what to do.

Panic-stricken, Amos crept unnoticed into the cottage. He could no longer bear to see his parents humiliated in this way. Things had to change for him and his family, and it was up to him to do something. He needed to act now. But what should he do? How could he and his parents hope to flee this kingdom that had become like a prison? He looked around, hoping to come up with an idea, a trick that would allow him to get rid of Edonf once and for all.

While waiting for him to return, Amos's mother had put some water in the pot above the fire. Frilla Daragon had looked forward to making a soup with whatever her son brought home. Amos had an idea, and he plucked up enough courage to act. To avoid burning himself, he wrapped a thick cloth around one of his hands, then grabbed the big pot by its handle. Unobserved, he went out to the garden, not far from Edonf and one of his men. He put the pot on the ground, took a dead twig in his hand, and began a strange ritual. He danced as he whipped the side of the pot with the twig.

"Come to a boil, my soup! Come to a boil!" he repeated with each blow.

Consumed by anger, Edonf did not pay attention to Amos right away. Only after the seventh or eighth "Come to a boil, my soup! Come to a boil!" did Lord Edonf stop his ranting long enough to watch what Amos was doing.

"What are you up to, you stupid boy?" he yelled.

"I'm boiling water for dinner, my good lord. We'll make

a soup from stones!" Amos answered, somewhat proud of himself.

Intrigued, Lord Edonf looked at Amos's parents, who just smiled slightly. They knew how quick-minded their son was and that he was cooking up something other than soup.

"And by what miracle can you make soup from stones?" asked Lord Edonf.

Amos had just hooked a big fish with his bait, and he wasn't letting it go. His trick seemed to be working only too well.

"It's very simple, my lord," he said. "With this magic wand, I'll bring the water to a boil and it will be warm enough to melt stones. When the mixture cools off, it will be smooth and deliciously creamy. This is the only nourishment that my parents and I have had for years."

Edonf laughed heartily. He raised one of his shirtsleeves and rapidly dipped his hand in the water to check the temperature. As soon as he felt the burn caused by the intense heat of the liquid, his face became livid and he removed his hand in a shriek of pain. The water was truly boiling! His hand as red as a lobster, Edonf jumped up and down as he cursed all the gods of heaven.

"Quick! Quick! Some cold water!" he shouted, stamping his feet violently. "Quick! Some ice water!"

One of the guards, who had gone off to inspect the little barn, ran out to help his master. Without hesitation, he took hold of Edonf's arm and, thinking the water was cold, dipped his hand in the pot again.

*"Let go of my hand, idiot! Let go of my hand or I'll have you hanged!"* Lord Edonf yelled, tears coming to his eyes.

The guard did not understand why he was being insulted, or why his master proceeded to beat him. Kicking his backside, Edonf shoved him to the ground. Amos's parents tried hard not to laugh. Meanwhile, Amos made a compress from the leaves of several plants and handed it to Edonf. The lord finally calmed down, exhausted by the mishap.

"I want the twig that can bring water to a boil," he said. "Give me this twig and I'll give you permission to farm whatever land you want and to hunt on my property. I'll even give you the donkey!"

Amos put on a very serious face. His heart was beating madly; he was afraid that Edonf would realize he was being duped, but he did not show his fear. He had to conduct the discussion skillfully.

"Unfortunately, my lord, this magic twig has been in my family for generations," Amos said. "It's our most precious belonging and my parents cannot afford to part with it. Forget you ever saw this twig. Burn the house; we'll go live elsewhere, far from your kingdom."

Edonf's face contracted with pain as he took ten gold coins out of his purse.

"Here is my offer for your magic stick. If you refuse this money, I'll take your twig regardless and have your house set on fire. It's up to you! Decide quickly, boy; I've almost reached the limits of my patience!"

Lowering his head as if in shame, Amos handed the stick to the lord.

"Your will prevails," he said. "Yet you should know that it's with a heavy heart that I accept this money. But please, my lord, don't forget to dance around the pot as you chant, 'Come to a boil, my soup! Come to a boil!' "

Edonf threw the gold coins onto the ground and grabbed the twig. "I'll remember. I'm not stupid," he said before climbing up on his horse.

In turn, the guards mounted their horses and the three men quickly disappeared.

Thanks to his cunning, Amos had earned the money needed to go to the woods of Tarkasis as he had promised Crivannia, princess of the waters.

But Amos was aware that Edonf would come back as soon as he discovered he had been duped. So he concocted a new plan. He made the donkey swallow eight of the ten gold coins, which he'd coated with hay and a laxative herb to facilitate their quick expulsion by the animal. He then told his parents of his adventure at the bay of caverns. To prove the truthfulness of his story, he showed them the white stone and the trident the mermaid had given him. Urban and Frilla understood right away the importance of the mission entrusted to their son. They were proud of him and encouraged Amos to go to the woods of Tarkasis to deliver Crivannia's message.

Twelve long and difficult years had passed since the time the Daragons had settled in Edonf's kingdom, and their survival instinct made them face the truth: Omain had nothing but poverty and misery to offer. It was time to leave. They did not possess much, so packing was done quickly.

"Go to the clearing by the foot of the mountain," Amos told his parents. "I'll meet you there and I'll bring horses."

Without questioning him, Urban and Frilla left right away

to go to the meeting place. Their arms loaded with parcels, they walked unconcerned for the son they left behind. Amos was endowed with a prodigious intelligence and he would know how to protect himself against Edonf's viciousness. The young boy had more than one bag of tricks with which to fool his enemies.

Amos waited patiently for Edonf's return, saying good-bye to the forest where he was born, to his little cottage, and to the donkey he would have to part with. As anticipated, it wasn't long before Edonf reappeared with his two guards.

*"I'll cut your head off, little swine!"* he shouted. *"I'll slash your belly open! I'll gulp you down in one bite, you louse!"*

Calmly and unnoticed by Edonf and his men, Amos went to the small barn. He grabbed the ears of the donkey and looked straight into its eyes.

"Donkey, give me some gold! Give me some gold!" he commanded.

Edonf and his guards went first into the cottage. They looked around quickly. Then, as they were rushing toward the barn, Amos's voice stopped them short. They heard him chanting, "Donkey, give me some gold!"

"Let's approach silently," said Edonf to his guards. "We'll take him by surprise."

The three men peered into the barn through the many gaps in the planks.

They saw Amos gently stroke the donkey's ears while repeating the same sentence: "Give me some gold! Give me some gold!"

Suddenly they saw the animal raise its tail and defecate.

They could not believe their eyes when, one by one, Amos extracted eight gold coins from the droppings. Edonf rushed into the barn.

"Little brat! You thought you fooled me with your fake twig to boil water, didn't you?" he said as he unsheathed his sword. "I made a mockery of myself in front of my court. A short while ago, all I could think of was killing you, but now I've a better idea. I'm going to take your donkey. I had heard that magic hens were able to lay golden eggs, something I never believed. But now I know that some donkeys can give gold too!"

Amos frowned. "Take my money, take my donkey and I hope you make it gallop to the castle! Then you'll upset its stomach and all he'll ever give you is dung!"

Edonf burst out laughing. "You think you're clever, don't you? Why, you just gave me the precious advice I need to keep from making a serious mistake. Guards, lead this donkey out with great care! We'll take it on foot to the castle. We'll leave the horses here and come back for them later. I'll walk behind you to make sure that no mishap endangers this precious creature. And if the animal poops on the way, I'll collect all the gold coins it drops. As for you, little vermin, you can keep the eight gold coins." He bent down to pick one up and tossed it back onto the ground. "They're still warm! Along with the ten others I've already given you for the twig, you can consider that payment for the donkey."

"No, please, my good lord, give me back my donkey!" Amos begged. "He's all we have. Kill me if you want, but leave the donkey to my parents."

Lord Edonf knocked Amos to the ground with a swift kick. "Why don't you eat stone soup? It's your specialty, isn't it?"

Amos watched as Edonf and his two guards walked away with the precious animal. The fat man was singing and laughing. Amos too was rejoicing.

He had played his part well. He mounted Edonf's horse and attached the two other horses' bridles to his own. Then he went directly to the clearing at the foot of the mountain where his father and mother were waiting.

And so a new tale spread in the kingdom of Omain. The elders still retold the legend of Yack the Troubadour, but now the children also wanted to hear the story of Amos Daragon, the clever boy who had bartered a simple twig for ten gold coins, and a plain donkey for three beautiful horses.

## —3—

# BRATEL-LA-GRANDE

Amos's parents had heard of the woods of Tarkasis. In the course of past travels, before their son's birth, rumors concerning the place had reached their ears. It was said that those who dared to enter this forest were never seen again. A terrible power was supposed to inhabit these woods. Urban Daragon told his son that when he had looked for work in the small town of Berrion, he had met a very old man in the marketplace. This man was desperately trying to find his lost childhood.

He would stop every passerby. "Madam! Sir! Excuse me!" he would say. "My childhood was stolen from me! I need to find it again! Help me, please. I beg you. I'm only eleven years old! Only yesterday I was a happy child. But when I woke up this morning, my childhood was gone. Help me! Please, help me!"

Some people laughed at this strange man; others ignored

him. No one took him seriously. Only Urban Daragon had ever approached him and asked what had happened to him.

"I lived close to the woods of Tarkasis," the white-bearded and white-haired old man had answered. "My parents owned a cottage at the edge of the forest. My father told me over and over not to venture near there. Yesterday morning, I lost my dog and went to look for it. As I searched around the house, I heard barking farther away. It was my dog. I recognized the way he barks when he's scared. I ran after him, giving no thought to my parents' warnings. I remember seeing a lot of light, like little spots of sun shining through the trees. Then out of nowhere, beautiful, soft music started to play, and suddenly I felt like dancing. I was waltzing with the lights, I was so happy. I was calm and peaceful. I don't know how long this lasted, but I probably danced for a very long time, because I fell asleep from exhaustion. When I woke up, there was no trace of my dog. I had this long white beard, and my hair had also turned white and grown a lot. Actually, all the hair on my body was white. Panicked, I hurried back to the house and realized that it had disappeared. So had my parents. The place was completely different, and a road stretched across where my father's vegetable garden used to be. In tears, I followed that road and arrived here, in Berrion. This town is just a few minutes from Tarkasis, and yet I didn't know of it. I had never heard of it. It's as if it sprouted suddenly during the night. I don't understand what is happening to me, dear sir. I'm eleven years old! We just celebrated my birthday. I swear that I'm not an old man. I'm not crazy. Please help me find my childhood again. Help me find my parents, my house, and my dog. Please, sir . . ."

Urban had believed the poor man, but there was nothing he could do for him. So he had gone on his way, shaken by the story he had heard.

ψ

The town of Berrion lay in the northernmost part of the country. After a night spent sleeping in a clearing, the Daragons got on their way at sunrise the next morning. They were ready for the monthlong journey. They had three good horses and ten gold coins. Amos had given eight of the coins to his father upon their reunion, and his father had carefully put them in his purse. Amos had hidden the other two coins in his shoes in case his trick with the donkey backfired. Edonf could have guessed that he had been tricked when Amos removed the coins from the animal's droppings. But since Lord Edonf was even stupider than the donkey, the Daragons were in a position to undertake a trip entirely financed by their former master.

As they went through the mountain pass, Amos, Urban, and Frilla left the kingdom of Omain. They followed the north road, crossing plains and valleys, several poor villages, some green forests, and many charming little farms. The journey seemed very long to Amos. He wasn't used to riding for entire days and went to sleep completely exhausted at night.

Along the way, Urban Daragon and his wife bought all they needed for their long trip: food, a tent, good blankets, and an oil lamp. Amos had never seen his father so happy or his mother so beautiful. Day by day, his parents were coming back to life. It was as if they were opening their eyes and awakening after an endless and gloomy slumber.

Frilla's soft hands often braided her son's hair with tender care. Urban laughed a lot, which touched Amos's soul, and, in spite of his fatigue, he felt a kind of happiness he had never known before.

Amos played with his father, washed himself in the clear water of small rivers, and enjoyed the excellent food cooked by his mother. He was also given a plate of black leather armor that she had made for him, and his father bought him an earring representing a wolf's head. Atop his horse, Amos looked majestic. With the mermaid's trident slung across his back, his long braided hair, and his tightly fitted armor, he looked like a young warrior out of an old tale. In spite of all their expenses, Urban's purse still contained six shiny coins—a huge fortune compared with the poverty that they saw around them.

By the fire at night, Urban spoke of his life, fascinating Amos with stories of his travels and adventures. He was an orphan and had learned a trade early in life to survive. He then took to the road "to conquer the world," as he said, laughing at his innocence. Unfortunately, he encountered more disappointments than satisfaction on his travels. But his fate turned the day he met Frilla. She was a beautiful eighteen-year-old girl, with her long black hair and nut-brown eyes, a shepherdess by trade. She won his heart. Her parents had promised her to another man, so she and Urban eloped. A happy star had appeared in the young man's life, and for eight years Urban and Frilla lived blissfully, wandering from village to village, from one kingdom to another. Then an even greater happiness befell them after they settled in the kingdom of Omain, the birth of their child. But the miserable twelve years that followed had been a horrible experience that they now wanted to forget.

Two weeks into their journey north, the Daragons met a knight on the road. He sported a large sword, his shield was adorned with a blazing sun, and his armor sparkled as bright as a mirror.

"Stop!" he shouted. "Identify yourselves, or you'll pay for your silence."

Urban Daragon cordially introduced himself and explained that he and his family were headed north to Berrion. He added that he and his wife were craftspeople who had decided to travel again after spending a good number of years in the kingdom of Omain, where their excellent workmanship had been rewarded many times by the ruler. It was not a common sight to see craftspeople riding such beautiful horses, but the knight nodded as if satisfied with the explanation. Of course, Urban did not confess the real reasons that were taking them to Berrion.

"Is it true that the lord of Omain is as stupid as an ass?" the knight inquired, laughing.

"It's an insult to donkeys to compare them to Lord Edonf," Amos answered. "At least donkeys are hardworking beasts. It would take only one knight such as yourself to seize all the land in Omain. The entire army there is just like Lord Edonf—cowardly and lazy."

"Your son has a sharp tongue, but he seems to recognize the power of the sword when it crosses his path," the knight said, obviously flattered by the compliment. "My fellow knights and I are on the lookout for sorcerers hiding by the roadside in this forest. We know they're in there, but they surely bear no resemblance to you. You may continue on your way, good travelers." The knight nodded. Then he added, "Be informed that you're entering the kingdom of the Knights of Light. Our capital, Bratel-la-Grande, is only a few miles away. Tell the sentinel at the city gates that Barthelemy gave you permission to enter. Don't waste time getting to the capital. When night falls, strange things happen outside our walls. May the light shine on you! Farewell, good people."

Along the way to Bratel-la-Grande, Amos and his parents passed through two small villages, where a heavy and threatening silence hovered in the air. In the streets, around the houses, everywhere, all they saw were stone statues—men, women, and children frozen in fright. Amos climbed off his horse and touched a man's face. It was smooth and hard, cold and lifeless. He was obviously the blacksmith. His arm was raised in midair, a hammer in his hand, and he seemed ready to strike something in front of him. His beard, hair, and clothes had been turned to stone. Several other people were similarly petrified in mid-motion; the rest were lying lifeless on the ground. Even dogs poised to attack were frozen.

Something or someone had come to these villages and cast a spell over every inhabitant. Terror was clearly visible on the faces of all these human statues. Pigs, chickens, mules, and cats had also been turned to stone.

Unexpectedly, a big gray tomcat, obviously very old, came out of a woodpile and moved slowly toward the travelers. He seemed to be sniffing the scent of the newcomers. Amos approached the animal. He took it in his arms and noticed right away that the cat was blind. Why hadn't this cat fallen under the spell? Amos wondered. The explanation seemed obvious: the cat's blindness had saved it, which meant that *looking* at the enemy had turned the people and animals to stone.

In fact, after taking a closer look, Amos realized that there wasn't simply one enemy; there were several. The ground was covered with many strange footprints: triangular footprints, ending with three long toes, were clearly visible all around. On closer inspection, Amos noticed that a membrane linked the toes together. These creatures likely stood on two legs, and were web-footed like ducks.

Urban entreated his son to mount his horse again. This place made him uneasy and the sun was about to set. Frilla held on to the blind cat that Amos had placed in her arms, and the family left this ill-fated place to go to the kingdom's capital.

Bratel-la-Grande was an impressive city. Built in the center of an agricultural plain, it was surrounded by high gray stone walls that made it impregnable to any army. All around the farmed lands was a huge forest. From the top of the lookout towers, the sentinels could easily detect an enemy a mile away. An imposing iron grate protected the huge city gates.

Five sentries, wearing shining armor and holding shields decorated with a radiant sun, stopped the travelers. Urban gave his name and mentioned Barthelemy, as the knight had advised him to do. The sentries seemed satisfied.

"The gates remain open during the daytime, so as a security measure we open the iron grate only twice a day, at sunrise and sunset," one of the sentries said. "The peasants who work the land nearby will return home soon, before the sun sets in an hour. You'll be able to enter into town with them. In the meantime, take a break. We have food and drink. Help yourselves—the food is on the large rock over here. Welcome to Bratel-la Grande, travelers! May the light shine on you!"

Grateful, the Daragon family thanked the sentry and went to the rock. Amos helped himself to an apple and some chestnuts and sat near the iron grate to look inside the town. There was a lot of activity, with citizens coming and going and knights patrolling the streets. It almost seemed as if the residents were getting ready for battle. In the town square, not far from the gates that the Daragons were soon to enter, ashes of what had been a large fire were still smoking. Amos asked one of the sentries why such a big fire had been lit in daylight.

"We burned a witch this morning," the sentry said. "You must have seen what happened in the villages you crossed. Our ruler, Yaune the Purifier, thinks we're dealing with the evil spell of a sorcerer. Our men are searching the forest to catch the culprit. All those who practice some kind of witchcraft are placed on the pyre and burned alive. Just this week, seven people have died in this manner, including a few humanimals."

Amos asked what a humanimal was. He had never heard the word.

"They're humans who are able to transform themselves into animals," the sentry explained. "When I was very young, people talked a lot about humanimals. Now it's more a legend than a reality." He shrugged. "I never believed those stories, and I doubt that the man and woman who died this morning had such an ability. Our ruler must feel very helpless. No one knows what is really happening in the kingdom. Every night, we hear awful noises coming from the forest. The residents don't sleep much. Everyone lives in fear when night comes. I don't know what to think of all this myself." He shook his head. "Well, it's time now to open the iron grate. Good-bye, young man. May the light shine on you!"

"May the light shine on you as well!" Amos answered.

The peasants entered Bratel-la-Grande, followed by the Daragon family. Urban, Frilla, and Amos immediately searched for a place to spend the night. They found an inn called the Goat's Head. It was a dark, disquieting place. The walls were gray and dirty. There were a few tables, a long bar, and several customers talking to each other. The atmosphere seemed sinister to the Daragons when they walked in. They knew full well that they were being stared at from head to toe.

A pleasant smell of warm soup wafted from the kitchen, and Amos was nearly drooling when they sat down at a table. The chatter started again and no one paid them any more attention. After a few minutes, Urban called the innkeeper over. The man did not move from behind the bar.

"There's a wonderful smell coming from your kitchen!" Frilla said, trying to get his attention. "We'd like to eat and sleep here tonight."

The man still did not budge. He simply went on talking with the other customers, not bothering to glance at the Daragons. When the family finally decided to leave, the innkeeper winked to his regular customers.

"One moment," he shouted. "You must pay before you head out!"

"We did not eat, we did not drink, sir," Urban answered. "So why should we have to pay?"

"Be informed that we don't wait on strangers here," the innkeeper said, beaming with satisfaction. "Yet you've enjoyed the aroma of my cooking, for which you must pay. Did you imagine that you could indulge your hunger and not give me a few coins?"

The other customers burst into laughter. Obviously they were used to hearing the innkeeper extort money from unsuspecting travelers.

"You must pay or go to jail!" the innkeeper went on.

Urban refused to open his purse. Three men got up, clubs in their hands, and went to block the exit.

"Go and bring back a knight," the innkeeper told one of his friends. "We have a problem here."

A few minutes later, the friend returned with a knight. It was Barthelemy.

"What is going on this time?" asked the weary knight as he walked in.

"These thieves want to leave without paying," said the innkeeper. "They inhaled the fragrance of my soup and refuse to pay for it. This is my inn and I can sell whatever I please, even a smell, isn't that so?"

Barthelemy recognized the Daragon family.

"You came to the wrong place, my friends," he told them. "This inn is probably the worst one in all of Bratel-la-Grande. According to our laws, this man is right; all travelers who stop at the Goat's Head are swindled in the same way. He uses our laws to his advantage. He's a crook and there is nothing I can do about it. I must make sure that this man is paid for the kitchen smells you enjoyed. I must also tell you that in case of a dispute, the knights will judge the case. I counsel you to give him something and leave. There is nothing I can do for you."

"Very well," Amos said with a sigh. "We will pay the innkeeper."

The whole assembly erupted in laughter again. The trick always worked, and the regular customers always watched the scene unfold with glee.

Amos took his father's purse. "We have exactly six gold coins," he told the innkeeper. "Will that be enough to pay for the scent of a soup that we did not taste?"

Delighted, the innkeeper rubbed his hands. "But of course, young man! It's the perfect sum!"

Amos shook the purse and jingled the coins close to the scoundrel's ear.

"Just as we inhaled the smell of a soup that we did not eat," he said, "now you are paid in kind with the sound of coins that you'll never pocket."

Barthelemy laughed loudly. "I believe that this boy has just settled his and his parents' debt right in front of my eyes!" he exclaimed.

The innkeeper stood openmouthed. He was humiliated. He had been outwitted by a child.

Amos and his parents left, accompanied by Barthelemy. As soon as they were outside the inn, all four of them laughed heartily. However, inside the inn, a profound silence had replaced the mocking laughter.

# —4—

## BEORF

At the suggestion of their new friend Barthelemy, Amos and his parents settled in a nice inn owned by the knight's mother. They were happy to be able to rest at last. The old blind cat they had adopted lost no time finding a cozy corner to sleep in.

Urban also found a job at the inn. The roof needed to be replaced. After his father's death, Barthelemy had become the inn's caretaker, but in spite of his goodwill, he wasn't very handy; Urban gladly agreed to take care of whatever needed to be fixed. To compensate him, a large, comfortable, sunny room was put at the Daragons' disposal. And since Frilla agreed to help in the kitchen, the family was also fed. This arrangement suited the Daragons, who quickly settled into their new dwelling.

The inn was named the Shield and the Sword. It was the favorite meeting place of the knights of Bratel-la-Grande.

They gathered there to drink, talk about their recent battles, and play cards. From sunrise to late in the night, there was always someone to narrate a warlike feat, boast about his exploits, or simply relax between two missions. Barbarians from the north regularly invaded the kingdom, and serious battles were commonplace. Barthelemy's father, who had been a great knight, had been killed in battle. His victories were still recounted often. He remained alive in the memory of his companions in arms, and the stories of his prowess moved his widow to tears every time.

When passing through Bratel-la-Grande, the knights of neighboring kingdoms always stopped at the Shield and the Sword to discuss the latest news and to boast of their dexterity with sabers. It was a lively spot, always swarming with people, where laughter and the most incredible stories could be heard at any time of the day.

The inn was spacious, well kept, and surrounded by magnificent rosebushes. Located a fair distance from the center of town, this dark redbrick two-story house had a lot of charm. Yaune the Purifier, lord of Bratel-la-Grande and master of the Knights of Light, often came here to relax or talk with his men. For someone as inquisitive as Amos, being in the hub of everything that was happening in the kingdom was a dream come true.

The knights often talked about the curse that had fallen over several of the villages. No one could explain how the residents had been transformed into stone statues. So as a measure of security, the knights had encouraged all villagers to evacuate to Bratel-la-Grande. Those who had not heeded the warnings fell victim to the terrible curse. In fact, the scourge struck everyone who spent the night outside the walls of the capital.

In town it was rumored that an army sent by a neighboring kingdom to lend a helping hand had been turned to stone in the forest. Cavalry detachments regularly saw stonelike owls, deer, and wolves. And from the depths of the forest, piercing shrieks were nightly occurrences that froze the blood of the residents. Every night the shrieks seemed to get a little closer to the fortified walls of the capital.

The knights had to confront an invisible enemy that hid deep in the darkness. This hostile force was so powerful that it seemed invincible. It was hard to believe that only one individual was responsible. But none of the victims was able to say a word about the physical appearance or motive of this unseen enemy. Like everyone else in town, Barthelemy and his companions were alarmed, and Yaune the Purifier seemed to be resorting to drastic measures when he burned supposed witches and magicians. It was hard to know how to fight this obscure danger that threatened all living creatures in the kingdom.

A week had gone by since Amos and his parents had arrived in Bratel-la-Grande. Although they enjoyed their surroundings, they knew that they had already spent too much time in town and so decided to resume their journey to the woods of Tarkasis.

The story of how Amos had outsmarted the innkeeper at

the Goat's Head had spread rapidly among the town's knights. Barthelemy particularly enjoyed telling his companions how a boy had rendered the dishonest innkeeper speechless. Strangers frequently bowed to Amos to congratulate him for putting the crooked man in his place.

Amos took long walks in town. He strolled along, casually discovering the small streets and the tiny shops of craftsmen. A large market was held every morning in the center of town, right in front of Yaune the Purifier's huge fortified castle. One day, as Amos stood in the marketplace, he saw a boy walking on all fours under the merchants' stalls. He was maybe a little older than Amos, as plump as a young pig, and had long straight blond hair. In spite of his large bottom and his rolls of fat, he moved with remarkable agility. Quick as lightning, his hands grabbed fruit, pieces of meat, sausages, and bread loaves without being noticed. Once his bag was full, the boy left the marketplace.

Curious, Amos decided to follow him. He noticed then that the young thief had thick sideburns. The boy quickly turned around a street corner and walked toward one of the town's fortified walls, located far from any dwellings. Once at the foot of the wall, he looked around furtively and promptly vanished. Amos could not believe his eyes. He approached the spot where the boy had stopped, and discovered a deep hole. The boy had likely jumped into the hole, which would explain his sudden disappearance.

In turn, Amos jumped into the hole. At the bottom he saw that a long tunnel had been roughly scooped out under the wall. He followed it and came out on the other side, in the high grass of the plain. Standing on his toes, Amos looked around, trying to spot the boy. He saw him for only one brief second before he disappeared again, at the far edge of the forest. How was it possible for such a heavy person to move so quickly? Amos wondered. In just a few minutes, the boy had crossed the field as fast as a galloping horse. Even more incredible was that he was still carrying his huge bag of stolen goods.

Running as fast as he could, Amos went to the edge of the forest. On the ground, under a canopy of trees, he noticed strange marks. These consisted of footprints—and also of handprints. Was the heavyset boy moving on all fours in the forest? Farther down, the prints changed to that of a young bear. Amos thought there was only one answer to this enigma: he had followed a humanimal. It was the only thing that could explain the boy's agility, strength, and speed. Young bears were fast and powerful creatures. It would also explain why the strange fugitive had so much hair on his face.

Amos rejoiced to think that humanimals were not legendary creatures after all. They really existed! There truly were humans capable of morphing into an animal at will. He knew that very few humans possessed this fantastic gift.

Amos remembered the two humanimals who the sentry had told him had been burned in the town square of Bratel-la-Grande. He reached the sad conclusion that a young person who steals food to survive probably has no parents to take care of him. And he knew that only one explanation was possible: the Knights of Light had killed this boy's parents. The knights had probably seen them change from humans to animals, and had wrongly assumed that if a human could transform himself or herself into a beast, he or she could also turn people to stone.

*I must find this boy and speak to him*, Amos decided.

With the mermaid's trident slung across his shoulder, Amos entered the forest and followed the humanimal's tracks. After an hour's walk, he reached a small clearing. The prints in the ground led him to a cozy round cottage made of wood. All around the house were many beehives, with thousands of buzzing bees.

"Is anyone home?" Amos shouted in a friendly manner. "Answer me. I don't come as an enemy. I followed your tracks, young bear, and I would very much like to talk to you."

No one replied. In fact, with the exception of the bees, Amos didn't hear a sound. He took the trident in one hand and carefully approached the house. To his surprise, it had no windows. He knocked on the door.

"My name is Amos Daragon! I would like to speak to someone!" he shouted again.

There was still no answer. Amos pushed the door open gently, took a look around the room, and went in slowly. A strong smell of musk—of a wild animal—hit his nostrils. On a stool, Amos saw the flickering light of a small candle. In the middle of the room, a dying fire was still smoking a little. Daylight came in through an opening in the center of the roof that let out the smoke of the fireplace. On a low wooden table were a piece of bread and a jar of honey. Near the door, close to him, Amos saw the large bag of food with its stolen contents.

Suddenly, in a great commotion, the table was whisked off its legs and went flying into the air. It crashed against a wall and came tumbling to the ground. At that instant, a blond-colored bear jumped over Amos and, seething with anger, pushed him out of the house with one paw. In less than a second, the beast was on top of him, crushing him with all his weight. As the bear was about to slash Amos's face with its razor-sharp claws, Amos got hold of his trident and pointed it at the animal's throat. With each one threatening to kill the other, both fighters stopped moving. The bees, now ready to fight, had gathered in a cloud right over the bear's head. Amos quickly realized that the animal exercised a power over the insects. The beast was growling orders to his flying army.

"I don't mean you any harm," Amos said calmly as he tried to engage the bear in dialogue. "I've come to talk to you about your parents. Please . . . you're crushing me."

To Amos's astonishment, the bear's body regained some of its human shape. Its head was now that of the boy at the market. But he kept the huge, sharp teeth of a beast. And his right arm, still in midair as if ready to strike, kept the form of a bear's paw, but his left arm had come back to normal and was pinning Amos against the ground.

"I don't trust you!" the humanimal said, even though the trident remained aimed at his throat. "I've seen you several times with the knights. You even live at an inn that belongs to one of them. I noticed you well before you knew I existed. You're a spy and I will kill you."

"Well, if you're going to kill me, get it over with. And since you know me so well, you must be aware that I am not from this realm and that I'm not a threat to you," Amos said. "I advise you to eat me quickly. But if you do, you'll never know what happened to your parents."

On a signal from the humanimal, the bees flew back to their hives. The bear then became completely human again. He abandoned his aggressive behavior and became a mere fat boy sitting on the ground. He started to cry softly.

"I know what the knights did to my parents," he said. "They believed that my mother and father turned all the villagers in the surrounding towns to stone. But I'm not a sorcerer and neither were my parents. I won't hurt you. Actually, I would rather have you kill me. That way, I'd be free of my sorrow."

As Amos got up, he noticed that his armor was ripped. The bear's claws had gone through the leather, leaving four long tears. Without that protection, Amos knew he would have been seriously injured.

"You're very strong!" Amos said. "Since you already know the fate of your parents, let me say how sorry I am. If there is anything I can do to help you, just let me know."

The boy seemed satisfied. He smiled. There was no trace of vengeance in his dark eyes. His chubby pink cheeks, his long blond side-whiskers, and his plump body made him instantly likeable. He would have looked like a normal boy were it not for the whiskers, the thick eyebrows that met above his nose, and the hair that covered the palms of his hands.

"This is the first time I've seen a human show any kindness to a humanimal," he said. "My name is Beorf Bromanson. Very few like me remain in the world. I belong to a people known as man-beasts. Some legends say that humanimals were the first beings on this planet. We had kings and magnificent realms in the depths of immense forests. Each family was linked in soul and in blood to an animal. There were man-dogs, man-birds, and a great number of creatures that had the ability to shape-shift into whatever they wanted to be. As for me, I come from the bear line. Sadly, humans never trusted us, and killed many of us. In fact, I've never met any other humanimal other than my parents. My father used to say that we were probably the last family in the bear line still alive on this earth. Now I'm probably the last of my race."

Amos suddenly thought that since Beorf lived in the forest, he might know something about the mysterious and wicked force that was wreaking so much damage in the realm. So he asked the humanimal whether he knew who or what was transforming the villagers into statues.

"I do know," Beorf said. "But it's a long story and I am too sad and too tired to talk about it now. Come see me tomorrow and I'll tell you all I know about those horrible creatures."

The two boys shook hands warmly. Amos was pleased to have met Beorf and promised to come back early the next day. He started off and was nearly in the thick of the forest when he heard the galloping of horses. He turned around and saw a dozen Knights of Light throwing a net over Beorf. Transformed into a bear, the humanimal was struggling to free itself of the trap. The bees were stinging the armored men furiously. One of the knights knocked Beorf out while another one set fire to the wooden house. Once the beast lay unconscious, the bees stopped their fight and returned to their hives.

In the net, the bear morphed into his human form. His feet

and hands were tied up before he was loaded onto a horse. Amos wanted to run to his aid, but he wisely thought that rather than confronting the powerful knights, it was best to find another way to try and save his friend. Hidden in the woods, he saw the knights take Beorf away. Huge flames were now consuming the cottage. The sight made Amos remember Beorf's words: "Sadly, humans never trusted us, and killed many of us."

Frantically he ran back toward Bratel-la-Grande.

# —5—

## THE GAME OF TRUTH

When Amos reached the capital, he was out of breath and exhausted. But he went straightaway to the Shield and the Sword. Barthelemy was at the inn, chatting with three other knights. They had all removed their armor and were applying ointment over the many bee stings that covered their skin. They had been stung everywhere: under their arms, behind their knees, in their mouths, even under their feet.

"Those bees are real devils! Look, they stung me on the palm of the hand I use to hold my sword," said one knight. "How's that possible? My hand was solidly around the handle of my weapon, and yet those blasted bees managed to sting me there!"

"That's nothing compared to what they did to me," complained another one. "Look at my right leg; it's almost paralyzed because of the swelling. I counted exactly fifty-three stings. And yet there is nothing on my left leg. Those bees knew exactly what they were doing by concentrating all their efforts to deprive me of one leg. An enemy on the ground is an enemy vanquished! Those little devils knew how to keep me down."

"And they stung me in the mouth and around the eyes," said the third one, with a lisp. "I can hardly see anything! At least I can still talk!"

Amos approached Barthelemy and told him that he wanted to speak with him in private. They moved away from the others.

"You made a mistake when you captured the young humanimal in the forest," Amos said. "He has nothing to do with the misfortunes that have befallen the realm, and he's the only one who knows something about the real enemy. You have to set him free!"

Barthelemy seemed surprised. "How do you know this? In any case, there is nothing I can do. He's going to be put to death tomorrow at sunrise."

"We have to save him," Amos insisted. "If there is nothing you can do, who should I speak to to gain his freedom?"

"Yaune the Purifier, my young friend!" declared the knight in a respectful tone. "He decreed that any person accused of witchcraft was to be put on the pyre. The knights obey their master and never criticize his orders. Humanimals are treacherous beings that deserve to die. Tonight you'll be able to attend the boy's trial. I advise you not to defend him. You could meet the same outcome and end up with him on the fire."

Amos asked Barthelemy what the trial consisted of, since it was evident that Beorf's fate had already been decided.

"The humanimal will be submitted to the game of truth. Yaune puts two pieces of paper in his helmet. The word 'guilty' is written on one, 'innocent' on the other. The accused draws one of the pieces of paper. His choice determines his guilt or innocence. I've never seen any accused pull out the piece that says 'innocent.' The light inspires Yaune the Purifier and he's never wrong. If your friend is innocent, the truth will come out and he'll be saved. But by my word as a knight, that would be the first time it has ever happened!"

Amos walked around the city as he waited for Beorf's trial. The market square had been transformed into a tribunal. In a few hours, the trial would start. His friend, imprisoned in a cage, was exposed to the eyes and insults of passersby. Some of them threw tomatoes and rotten eggs at him. Beorf fumed silently but his hatred and disdain were clear. Amos met his gaze and gave a quick nod.

Why did it always have to be this way? Amos wondered. Why was ignorance always pushing humans to imprison innocent people, to humiliate them publicly, and to threaten to execute them? Maybe Beorf would be placed on the pyre as his parents had been, condemned without any proof of wrongdoing. And all the villagers gathered in the town square were already salivating at the thought of the upcoming spectacle. Didn't they have any compassion? Hadn't this town, under the pretext of protecting itself, killed enough innocent victims? It seemed they needed still another, and probably more, to satisfy their appetite for blood. All these knights thought they were doing the right thing; none looked farther than the tip of his nose to question his actions. Amos, his stomach upset and his heart constricted, felt suddenly nauseated. He threw up behind the dilapidated wall of a deserted house.

An impressive crowd was assembling in the town square when Amos returned. He started pacing up and down, his brain working at full speed. He had to save his new friend, but how? Unable to explain why, he was convinced that Yaune the Purifier's game of truth was a mere ruse to instill fear in those he ruled. But what was the trick?

Amos picked up two stones of the exact same size but of different colors and put them in his pocket. The darker stone represented the word "guilty," the pale one the word "innocent." After ten tries, Amos drew the pale stone six times, the darker stone four times. Again and again he tried, with much the same results. But not once did Amos pick the same stone ten times in a row. So he concluded that it was impossible that Yaune's game of truth could be fair. According to Barthelemy, there had been many trials and none of the accused had ever won their freedom. They had all been found guilty, which went against all logic.

Suddenly everything became clear in Amos's mind. If every accused person invariably chose the word "guilty," it had to be because the word was written on both pieces of paper! Clearly, Yaune was a player who lied and cheated. It was the only explanation. Now Amos had to figure out a way to prove the lord of Bratel-la-Grande's treachery so Beorf could go free.

The trial was set to start and Amos was still looking for an answer to his problem. When he threw the dark stone on the ground for the last time, he hit upon a crystal clear solution. He laughed. He had just found a way to liberate his friend.

ψ

Yaune the Purifier moved toward the dais. He was a tall man of about sixty years. His long gray hair was gathered in a ponytail, and he had a thick gray beard. A long scar went from his right eye down to his upper lip. His armor was the color of gold. Two white wings adorned the sides of his helmet, and around his neck he wore a long chain with a big skull-shaped pendant. The skull was carved out of a green stone, with two eyes that seemed to be huge diamonds. Yaune was an imposing ruler, and his solemn expression commanded respect.

The crowd was agitated, milling and feverish. The gates of Bratel-la-Grande had been closed for the night, and all the knights were present. Under a thunderous round of applause, Yaune the Purifier started to speak.

"We are gathered here so that the light will triumph once more. Dear citizens of Bratel-la-Grande, the boy that you see before you in this cage is a sorcerer. Several knights witnessed his transformation into a beast. A knight never lies, and the word of my men cannot be doubted. The magic of this sorcerer is powerful, and just like the others we've caught, he will be condemned to the purifying fire so that our realm can be saved. That is, of course, unless the game of truth proves his innocence. Only if we eliminate all forms of witchcraft will we overcome the curse that is upon us. Truth and light are our guides and until now our intuitions have been just and our actions courageous. If any among you doubts the guilt of the young sorcerer, let him be heard now or forever be silent!"

A deep silence fell over the crowd.

"I would like to be heard," Amos shouted as he raised his hand. His shaky voice betrayed his nervousness. "I know that you are mistaken!"

The eyes of the crowd were immediately upon him, a boy who dared to question the word of the Knights of Light and Yaune the Purifier.

"Quiet, young man!" ordered Yaune. "Your youth and lack of experience are the excuse for your impertinence. Now withdraw your words or you'll pay dearly for them!"

"I maintain what I just said, sir," Amos answered as he regained some confidence. "This boy is called Beorf and he's my friend. He belongs to the race of humanimals. He's not a sorcerer and does not turn people into statues. I believe that if you burn this boy, you will never understand what is happening in your realm. He is the only one who has seen the creatures who threaten your safety. He's innocent of the crimes you accuse him of!"

For the first time during his rule, Yaune the Purifier was being challenged.

"Do you think, little weasel, that you are wiser than the lord of Bratel-la-Grande?" Yaune demanded to know. "For nearly forty years I have fought the occult forces of this world. I have given my blood for the truth. I have lost men, even whole armies. I have sacrificed a great deal to see man's light prevail over the world of darkness. Approach the dais so I can see you better."

Amos came closer, with dignity and in silence. Yaune smiled at the boy with the long braid, the torn leather armor, and the trident over his shoulder. Barthelemy intervened.

"Excuse him, great lord," the knight said, kneeling in front of Yaune. "I know this boy. He is foolish and doesn't know what he's doing. He lives with his parents at my mother's inn. They're travelers who recently arrived here. His father and his mother know nothing of his behavior. Forgive him and I will vouch for him."

Yaune looked down at his knight. "Very well, valiant Barthelemy. Your father saved my life several times and I owe you the same respect that I had for him. Take this boy away and make sure that I don't see him again at Bratel-la-Grande."

A man stepped out of the crowd. "Lord, my name is Urban Daragon. I know my son better than anyone else. I can assure you that if Amos says that your prisoner is innocent, he's right. Barthelemy is a good man, and I understand his desire to protect travelers whom he has befriended. The Daragon family thanks him with all their hearts, but I have always taught my son to act according to his convictions. May I also add that Amos is not foolish and that many would gain by listening to what he has to say."

Yaune quickly dismissed Barthelemy with a gesture of his hand. "Let the will of the father prevail! We will see to it that justice is done. I will subject the boy to the game of truth. We'll play for the fate of the young sorcerer. I will put two pieces of paper in my helmet. On one will be written the word 'innocent,' on the other the word 'guilty.'" Yaune looked at Amos. "You must draw one of the papers at random. If you choose the paper with the word 'innocent,' I'll spare the life of your sorcerer friend. But if you choose the paper that says 'guilty,' three of you will be put on the pyre—the young sorcerer, your father, and you. Those who dare come to the defense of Yaune the Purifier's enemies are traitors who deserve death. This will teach your father that it's better to follow the rules of the master than one's own convictions. Bring me two pieces of paper so I can get started!"

As Yaune wrote on the pieces of paper, Amos nodded discreetly at Beorf.

"I abide by the rules of this realm and I'll gladly play the game of truth," Amos said. "Allow me, though, to see what you wrote on the two pieces of paper before you put them in your helmet."

Yaune seemed surprised by this request but quickly pulled himself together.

"Enough nonsense and foolishness," he declared. "I am a knight. I do not lie or cheat. Approach the dais and let the truth shine on everyone's life."

The uneasiness shown by the lord of Bratel-la-Grande strengthened Amos's belief that he had written "guilty" on both pieces of paper. He could see it in the old man's eyes. As for Urban Daragon, he was perspiring heavily as he hoped that his son would come up with a way to spare them from the pyre. Barthelemy too was anxiously watching the scene, sure that he would witness the death of his friends the next morning. And Beorf, who was holding his breath, could not believe that Amos was putting his own life and that of his father on the line to save him, a humanimal that everybody despised. The crowd was calm, certain of the outcome of the game. Never had the lord of the realm made a mistake, and no one doubted that there would be a big fire in Bratel-la-Grande the following day.

Amos calmly dipped his hand inside the helmet. Then, in a flash, he grabbed one of the pieces of paper, popped it in his mouth, and swallowed it.

"What are you doing, you fool?" Yaune hollered.

Amos smiled. "It's simple enough," he said. "I took one of the pieces of paper and ate it."

The crowd snickered, angering Yaune. "But why did you do that, you stupid boy?" he raged.

Amos answered solemnly. "Now that I've eaten the paper I chose, no one here knows if my friend is innocent or guilty. To find out, all we have to do is look at the paper that remains in the helmet. If the word 'innocent' is written on it, it means that I ate the paper with the word 'guilty.' Therefore you'll burn us early tomorrow morning. On the other hand, if the word 'guilty' is written on the paper in the helmet, it means that I ate the paper with the word 'innocent.' So we'll be saved! Now I'd like Barthelemy to come up and read the verdict of your game of truth."

The knight approached and took the remaining paper out of the helmet. At the top of his lungs, he shouted, "Guilty."

Amos spoke again. "This proves that I ate the paper with the word 'innocent' written on it—unless, of course, your helmet contained two pieces of paper with the word 'guilty.' But I don't think that the leader of the Knights of Light is a cheater. Therefore the truth has just been declared."

The crowd applauded wildly, while Yaune hastily got up.

"The truth spoke. Free the boy in the cage," he said, his face red with anger. He leaned in close to Amos's ear and whispered, "You will pay for your trick. No one upsets the lord of Bratel-la-Grande without suffering consequences."

## —6—

## BANISHED

Amos went back to the inn, accompanied by his father and Beorf. A full, clear moon softly illuminated Bratel-la-Grande. Frilla and Urban welcomed the young humanimal as a son. During their meal, Amos explained to his parents how he had met Beorf in the forest. He also told them that the knights had captured the Bromansons and burned them on the pyre.

Worried, Frilla suggested that they leave Bratel-la-Grande as soon as possible. After all, their goal was to reach the woods of Tarkasis, and staying in town any longer seemed like a bad idea. They decided that they would be on their way at sunrise. Beorf would go with them. They still had enough money, and the horses had had plenty of time to rest.

Beorf then began to tell them what he had seen in the forest. He stopped suddenly and stared at the cat the Daragons had taken in.

Amos smiled. "Don't pay any attention to the cat," he said.

"He's not dangerous. We found him in one of the villages before we arrived here. He was the only creature that hadn't been turned into stone. Probably because he's blind. We took pity on him and adopted him."

Beorf whistled to attract the cat's attention and threw him a piece of meat from his plate. The cat jumped to catch it.

"As you can see, this animal isn't blind!" Beorf said. "Don't trust the way his eyes look. I tell you, he's not normal. Something about him makes me wary. I have a sense about these things when it comes to animals. I can feel their malicious intentions. This cat isn't honest. It pretends to be blind when in fact it's watching us and listening to everything we say."

To calm her guest, Frilla took the cat upstairs and locked him in her room. She looked carefully at the eyes of the animal before putting him on her bed. The cat was definitely blind. Two large cataracts covered its eyes. After her thorough inspection, she was convinced that the young humanimal was mistaken, and she came back down to sit at the table. Beorf resumed telling them what he had seen in the forest.

"They were women. Their bodies were monstrous and powerful. They had wings on their backs and long claws on their feet. Their heads were huge and totally round. They had greenish skin, large noses, and teeth that stuck out like boars'. On top of that, these creatures had forked tongues hanging out the sides of their mouths. I saw a blazing gleam in their eyes. When I looked at them, I wondered what was keeping their hair in constant motion. I almost died when I realized that it wasn't hair writhing on their heads but dozens of snakes! These hideous creatures are nocturnal, and they're always screaming in pain because the snake-hairs constantly attack their shoulders and backs. The sores ooze a dark liquid, thick and sticky. What I also know is that as soon as other living creatures lock eyes with them, they're turned instantly to stone."

"But tell me something," Amos said. "How do you know about the blazing gleam in their eyes if those who look at them are transformed into statues? Shouldn't you have been petrified too?"

The question seemed to surprise Beorf. Indeed, he should have been subjected to the same fate as the other men, women, and animals. He took a few seconds to remember what had happened, then explained how he had met up with these monsters.

"I was picking wild fruit near a village when night caught up with me. I went to sleep in the still-warm grass. The screams of the panicked villagers woke me up. I morphed into a bear and went closer to the houses to see what was causing such terror. I hid behind the forge and peeped through a hole in the wall, but I couldn't see things head-on. Then I noticed a large mirror in the blacksmith shop. The knights probably used it when they tried on new armor. The Knights of Light are so arrogant that if they could ride their horses with a mirror in front of them, all the better to admire themselves, they would. In any case, thanks to this mirror, I managed to see the creatures clearly—to see their reflections—without becoming a statue. I realize today that I was lucky to come out alive!"

"Now that we know what these beasts look like," said Frilla,

"I would like to know what they want and why they attack this realm and its inhabitants."

Amos yawned. "At least we know how to avoid becoming statues," he said. "What's more, it's obvious that—"

"Hush! Keep quiet!" Beorf whispered, grabbing his friend's arm. "Look slowly at the beam above your head. Your blind cat is spying on us."

Every member of the family looked up toward the ceiling at the same time. The cat was perched on a beam directly over the table, where it seemed to be listening to the conversation.

"You see, I was right," Beorf said. "This animal has ears too big and eyes too round to be a mere domesticated cat. As soon as it comes down from the beam, I'll take care of it! I'm sure that this dirty fleabag works for those monstrous creatures."

At that precise moment, Barthelemy walked in, accompanied by five other knights. He came over to the Daragons' table.

"By order of Yaune the Purifier, lord and master of Bratel-la-Grande," he announced, "we are here to evict Amos Daragon and his friend Beorf Bromanson from the city. I am very sorry to have to do this, but I must obey orders. Fellow knights, take them away!"

Urban rushed forward, trying to prevent the knights from taking his son. He received a powerful blow to the back of his head and lost consciousness. Begging for mercy, Frilla did her best to convince Barthelemy to spare her son. Amos would be easy prey for the creatures that had Bratel-la-Grande under siege if he was left outside the town walls at night. But

Barthelemy refused to hear the woman's pleas. Beorf was about to take his bear form and fight for his life, but Amos gave him a reassuring nod, which convinced him to calm down. When the knights and their two prisoners left the inn, the cat jumped from the beam to the windowsill; as quick as lightning, it disappeared into the night through a broken windowpane.

The two huge wooden gates and the iron grate were opened. Once the knights pushed Amos and Beorf out of the city, the gates were closed again. Amos and Beorf were left to fend for themselves.

"Let's try to think, my friend," Amos said. "We need a hiding place! I am only slightly familiar with the fields surrounding the city, and not at all with the forest. It's up to you to get us out of here before the snake-haired creatures sink their claws into us."

"I know where to go," Beorf said. "Climb onto my back and hold on tight!"

As he said these words, the young humanimal morphed into a bear. Amos jumped on his back and gripped his fur tightly. In less than a second, they were on their way. Although it was dark, Beorf ran quickly. He knew the area well enough to avoid obstacles and easily found his way.

After running through the forest for a good while, Beorf reached the foot of a gigantic tree, and once Amos slid off his back, he became human again. Perspiring, he lay down, his back against the ground and his plump stomach bulging. It took him a few minutes to catch his breath.

"Let . . . us . . . go down . . . quickly!" he managed to say at last.

Beorf dug at the ground with his hands until a trapdoor appeared. One after the other, the two friends climbed down a ladder that took them underground, directly beneath the tree. When they reached the bottom of the hole, they were enveloped in total darkness. Beorf groped around for a lamp, which he soon found.

"Take a good look, Amos; I'm about to perform a magic trick!" Beorf said.

He grunted softly, a sort of moan coming out of his chest. Amos looked up and saw many small lights entering through the open trapdoor. Above their heads, dozens, then hundreds of fireflies were swirling around. They descended suddenly toward Beorf and gathered inside the big glass lamp he was holding in his hand. This was how light filled the underground room, which was in fact a library.

The four walls were covered with books. Tall ones, short ones, fat ones, skinny ones—there were books everywhere. A large desk and a comfortable chair occupied the center of the room. In one corner lay a heap of hay and some blankets to be used as a bed. Beorf went up the ladder to close the trapdoor.

"This hiding place is safe—no one will find us here," he said. "Welcome to my father's lair. He was a fanatical reader. Always studying. You'll find books on everything. Some are written in strange languages that I can't understand. Feel free to look at them. As for me, I'm dead tired and I'm going to sleep. If you want the fireflies to turn off their lights, you just have to grunt three times. Good night, Amos."

Beorf had barely lain down on the floor before he started snoring. Amos walked around the room, looking at the books. There must have been more than a thousand. Some were old and dusty; others seemed more recent. Amos noticed that one book was sticking out from one of the shelves. It was an old book, transcribed by hand; its title was *Al-Qatrum, the Territories of Darkness*. Amos took it, sat down at the desk of Beorf's dead father, and started to read.

The book talked about a region located on the Hyperborean border, a world hidden in the earth's belly, where the sun never shines. It was the lair of the creatures of night, the birthplace of a race of monsters who had dispersed on the earth's surface.

To his great surprise, Amos came across a drawing representing the exact creatures Beorf had described at the inn. They were called gorgons. Their origins seemed to date far back in time. Long ago, Princess Medusa, a lovely young woman, had ruled over one of the islands of the Hyperborean great sea. Her beauty was such that Phorcys, the god of the waters, had fallen madly in love with her. Ceto, Phorcys's sister, wanted to keep her brother's love for herself and transformed Medusa into a repulsive and dangerous creature. To be sure that Phorcys would never meet Medusa's gaze again, she gave the princess the power to transform into stone any living being that looked into her eyes. Each time one of Medusa's snake-hairs bit her, the drop of blood that fell on the ground immediately became a snake that years later would change into a gorgon. It seemed that Medusa's beautiful island still existed and was inhabited by stone statues.

Amos closed the book. Now that he knew the history of these monsters, he had to find the reason why they were attacking villagers within the realm of the Knights of Light. No doubt Beorf's father had been trying to clear up this mystery before his death. If the book had not been put back in its proper place, it was probably because he had looked at it recently. Searching the desk drawer, Amos discovered Mr. Bromanson's notes. On a sheet of paper, he saw a drawing of the skull pendant worn by Yaune the Purifier. Wishing to further his research, Amos continued to read.

According to Beorf's father, Yaune the Purifier had stolen this sacred relic in his youth. At that time, he was called Yaune the Agitator. In a faraway land, he had attacked a village of sorcerers with his knights and had stolen this valuable object of black magic from a sacred temple. The pendant belonged to a cruel magician of darkness, who had been looking for it ever since. Only one of the Knights of Light had returned safe and sound to Bratel-la-Grande—none other than Yaune. He had set out as Yaune the Agitator and had been renamed Yaune the Purifier after boasting that he had vanquished all his enemies. As Yaune the Purifier, he had also been designated lord and ruler of the capital.

*Everything is clear,* Amos thought. *Barthelemy's father must have died during this battle. The gorgons are at the service of this magician of darkness, and as long as he does not get his pendant back, the city and its villages will remain in danger. I understand now why Yaune burns all magicians caught by his knights. He's afraid. He knows that he does not have what it takes to fight the sorcerer.*

Amos felt as if someone were watching him, and raised his head. In the darkness of the trapdoor, close to the ladder, he saw the blind cat looking at him. The animal took a few steps back and disappeared into the shadows.

## —7—

## THE DRUID

Amos had a hard time falling asleep. The gorgons, the skull pendant, Yaune, the cat in particular—all of them swirled in his head and made him think somber thoughts. When he woke up in the morning, he saw that Beorf had laid out breakfast on his father's desk. There were nuts, honey, wild fruit, bread, milk, and cakes. A soft light came into the library through a round window in the ceiling. Amos could not believe his eyes.

"Where did you find all this?" he asked.

"I've got my hiding places," Beorf answered as he swallowed a big piece of bread dripping with honey.

Amos took his first meal of the day with his friend. He explained in detail what he had discovered in Beorf's father's work. Then he told him about what had happened at the bay of caverns, his departure from the realm of Omain, and his journey with his parents to Bratel-la-Grande. Amos took the mermaid's white stone out of the little bag that served as a pocket inside his armor. He placed it on the table.

"Look, I must go to the woods of Tarkasis to hand this stone to someone named Gwenfadrille. I'm supposed to tell her that her friend Crivannia, princess of the waters, is dead and that her realm has fallen into the hands of the merriens. I must also tell her that Crivannia chose me to be the mask wearer. If only I knew what that means. I don't understand any of it."

Just as Amos finished talking, the blind cat jumped from the highest shelf of the library and landed directly on the table. He grabbed the stone between his teeth and rushed toward the exit.

"I'm going to reduce you to pulp," Beorf shouted after it. "You creepy animal!"

He morphed into his bear form and set off in pursuit of the cat, who shot up the ladder and slipped through the trapdoor. Beorf fell twice as he tried to climb after it. The first time, he fell on his backside; the second time, on his nose. The third time, he made it. Amos quickly grabbed his belongings, stuck the book *Al-Qatrum, the Territories of Darkness* under his arm, slung his trident over his shoulder, and climbed the ladder himself. Once outside, he followed Beorf's pawprints. The trail led straight to Bratel-la-Grande.

To Amos's surprise, the portcullis that protected the city was still open in spite of the mid-morning hour. But there were no peasants in the fields. Immediately Amos expected the worse. When he entered the capital, his fears were confirmed. He was aghast to see that all the dwellers had been turned to stone. The curse had spared no one.

Amos ran toward the Shield and the Sword. On his way, he met only petrified beings, their faces marked by fright. At the inn's door he was confronted by a painful sight—a motionless Barthelemy. Amos looked in vain for his parents. He kept hoping that he would find them safe and sound: Urban and Frilla knew the power of the gorgons and had no doubt escaped in time. But when he heard the shouts of a bear in distress, he remembered Beorf and hurried in the direction of the marketplace.

The humanimal was the prisoner of huge roots. They were wrapped around his paws, body, and throat. Amos didn't understand what had happened. How could roots have grown so fast as to immobilize his friend? Taking hold of his trident, Amos tried to free Beorf, when suddenly the voice of an old man stopped him.

"It's no use trying to liberate your friend, Mr. Daragon. The strength of one root is equal to the power of the druid who made it grow. And although I don't want to brag about it, a dozen or more woodcutters using heavy axes would not be able to cut these roots off."

Amos turned his trident nervously toward the man. His challenger had a long and dirty gray beard. His hair was also very long and tangled with twigs, dead leaves, and hay. He was wearing a brown robe, stained and threadbare. Wooden clogs, a belt made of braided vines, and a long twisted walking stick completed his attire. A huge red mushroom was growing from his neck, and his hands were covered with the kind of moss that usually covers boulders. The blind cat was at his feet, rubbing his head against the man's legs.

"Stop threatening me with your weapon, young man! You scare me! Oh! You scare me so much!" the old druid said, laughing. "Let us talk a little instead. I must know if you are worthy of the trust Crivannia put in you before she died."

Amos was not listening to him. "Your cat stole my white stone and I want it back right now!" he yelled.

The old man seemed surprised by Amos's assertive tone. "Mr. Daragon is very demanding," he snickered. "He gives me orders and threatens me with his ivory trident! It is indeed a dangerous weapon, but since it's obvious that you don't know how to use it properly, I don't fear for my life."

The druid opened his hand and Amos saw that the white stone lay between his dirty fingers.

"You already know my cat, I think," the druid went on. "I've been observing you through his eyes for quite a while. You're clever, my dear boy. I can feel your question coming: Why is this cat sometimes blind and sometimes not? Good question, Mr. Daragon! I'll answer you now. When I look through his eyes, he's not blind. It's as simple as that. One more question? Yes! Am I the magician of darkness who looks for his pendant and reigns over the army of gorgons? No, Mr. Daragon, I told you, I am a druid. A druid who's a little bit dirty, I reckon; a druid who does not always smell good, I agree; but I'm not nasty and I don't work for the forces of darkness. Neither do I work for the forces of light. You'll understand later on. Ah, really! You've another question! What am I doing here, at this hour and on this very day in the center of a city where people are now statues and with your white stone in my hand? I'll come to that. In the meantime, be patient! It's your turn to answer my questions. I want to know if you're intelligent enough to become a mask wearer."

"Free Beorf first," Amos demanded. "Then I'll answer your questions."

The druid smiled. His teeth were yellow, rotten, and wobbly. With a twitch of his nose, the old man called off the curse in order to gain Amos's trust. The roots that had ensnared the humanimal fell softly to the ground and dried up instantly.

"Think fast, young friend," said the old man. "What goes over a house once and not twice?"

"Simple! An egg," Amos answered without hesitating. "Thrown by someone, it could easily fly over a house, but I doubt that it could jump anywhere but in a frying pan after landing."

The old man seemed surprised by Amos's confident answer.

"I always start with an easy one to warm up a bit," he went on. "The next one is more difficult. What animal can go over a house but cannot cross a puddle of water?"

"You think that's more difficult?" Amos burst out laughing. "It's much easier than the other. An ant, of course."

The druid was becoming agitated. He had never met someone endowed with such a quick mind.

"Good luck with this one!" he said. "What goes around wood without ever entering it?"

"The bark," Amos answered, sighing with exasperation. "Too easy, much too easy!"

"The next is my best one! Listen carefully!" the druid went on, sure of the difficulty of his next riddle. "What gives shade in the forest without ever being there?"

Amos laughed. "The sun gives shade in the forest without ever being there! Since you think that you're so clever, answer this: The more of them there are, the less it weighs: what is it?"

The druid thought for a moment. "I don't know," he admitted. "What is it?"

"I'll tell you after you explain to me what you're doing here."

"You swear you'll tell me, Mr. Daragon?" inquired the old man anxiously.

"You have my word!" Amos answered.

"Very well, then, very well. To make a complicated story simple, I came here to look into the events of the past few weeks, specifically related to Yaune the Purifier and the pendant. I was much helped by what you read yesterday. I was reading the same lines as you were through the eyes of my cat. My druid order is of the opinion that the pendant is dangerous and that it ought not to fall into the wrong hands. This is why, when Yaune and his army were turned to stone during the night, I stole his pendant—so the gorgons could not hand it over to their master. As you can see, Mr. Daragon, I'm a powerful druid, but I must not in any way be implicated directly in this affair. I'm a magician of the realm of nature and not a mask wearer. My role is to protect animals and plants, not humans. In this world, two powers are constantly clashing: good and evil, what we call the powers of light and the powers of darkness. From the beginning of time, since the sun and the moon shared the earth, these two powers have been in endless conflict. The mask wearers are humans chosen for their spiritual and intellectual qualities. Their mission is to restore a balance between day and night, between good and evil. Since it's impossible to get rid of the sun or the moon, balance has to triumph. Mask wearers disappeared from this world hundreds of years ago. If Crivannia chose you, it's because she wanted to make you the first of a new generation of warrior men. Your task is to reestablish a fair balance in the world. A huge conflict is brewing. Already the merriens have attacked the mermaids, and soon they'll seize the oceans. Go as fast as you can to the woods of Tarkasis. Here is your stone back. I entrust you with Yaune's pendant as well. It is for you to decide whether to return it to its owner or not. It's your task, not mine. We will surely meet again. Now, may I have the answer to your riddle?"

"I'll tell you, but before I do, explain to me what a mask wearer is," Amos asked.

"I can't answer you, Mr. Daragon," the druid said sadly. "The more of them there are, the less it weighs: what is it?"

"Holes in a wooden plank," Amos answered.

The old man laughed heartily and beat on his tummy.

"That's a good one! Better than any of mine! I'd never have thought of it! Holes in a wooden plank! It's obvious, the more holes there are, the less it weighs! Take the pendant and the stone. My cat will keep an eye on you. Good-bye and good luck!"

Still laughing, the druid headed toward one of the big trees and vanished through the trunk. Beorf, who had regained his human form, came near his friend and put his arm across Amos's shoulders.

"I think we're in trouble," he said as he stroked the pendant with the tip of his forefinger.

Amos didn't know what to do. The situation was beyond him.

"I'm out of tricks, Beorf. I don't know what I'm supposed to do with this white stone. And I don't know what to do with this horrible pendant. My parents have disappeared and I have no idea where they could be. I've been chosen as a mask wearer, a job I don't understand." He sighed. "According to the druid, my ivory trident is a powerful weapon that I don't know how to use efficiently. And soon an army of gorgons led by an evil sorcerer will be chasing us. We're in the middle of a capital populated by statues, and I feel sure that the gorgons will come back tonight to search the place. What is to be done to bring balance between good and evil? Is there a way to reverse the curse and bring the people of the realm back to life? They're paying dearly for the theft of this pendant, and they don't deserve to remain statues for eternity. I don't know where to begin or what is the best way to get out of this mess."

Beorf nodded. "Let's try to analyze the situation calmly," he said. "Your mission is, first, to go to the woods of Tarkasis. That's what you have to do before anything else. If you leave with the pendant, the gorgons will follow you, and curse each of the villages you pass through. I believe that they can feel the pendant's presence and power. We could try to destroy the pendant, but it may hold some power that we might need. In fact, the magician of darkness came here to retrieve his pendant, and we can't allow him to leave this territory. I'll leave signs of my presence and of his piece of jewelry. This will force the sorcerer to remain within the borders of the realm. We have to find out who he is, where he's hiding, and how to get rid of him."

Amos didn't respond. He was thinking.

"We'll go our separate ways," Beorf continued. "I'll stay here with the pendant. I'm familiar with the fields and the forest. I can hide so that the gorgons won't find me. And I'll protect the pendant while you go seek more information about the white stone, about your trident, and about your mission. If you leave now, you'll have time to get out of the realm before nightfall. Trust me, this is the best plan."

Amos did not want to leave his friend to face danger alone, and he tried to find another solution, but Beorf's arguments were solid. Splitting up was the most logical thing to do. So he entrusted the pendant to Beorf and went to the Shield and the Sword to pick up his belongings. Since all the horses had been turned to stone, Amos set out on his journey on foot.

"Well, I'd best be on my way, Beorf," he said as he took leave of his friend. "Be very careful."

Beorf smiled. He transformed his right hand into a bear's paw and displayed his impressive claws.

"Leave the gorgons to me!" he said.

## —8—

## THE OLD WOMAN'S EGG

Nearly two weeks had gone by since Amos had left Bratel-la-Grande. The journey had been long and exhausting. Not knowing where the woods of Tarkasis were to be found, Amos had to stop and ask many people. Most had never heard the name, or, when they knew something about the woods, it was because of a tale or legend. So Amos went from village to village, sometimes traveling with merchants on their wagons, sometimes with troubadours who were too busy singing and didn't pay much attention to his questions.

More often alone than with company, Amos had to fend for himself to find things to eat, either in the forest or at peasants' homes, where he was given food and lodging in exchange for a day's work in the fields. Mostly he slept by himself in the forest or on the side of seldom-traveled paths. Each day, Amos felt increasingly helpless and regretted that his friend Beorf was not with him. He often thought that leaving Bratel-la-Grande on his own had been the wrong decision.

Disturbing rumors were spreading everywhere. Among them, it was said that the Knights of Light were under a terrible curse and that their realm was to be avoided at all costs. Villagers were suspicious of strangers and not very welcoming. Amos recognized himself in one of the rumors that warned of a boy who was traveling without his parents. As a result, a lot of people were suspicious of him and plied him with questions.

Amos's only distraction during his long trip to the woods of Tarkasis was the time he spent reading *Al-Qatrum, the Territories of Darkness*. The book was actually an encyclopedia of the harmful creatures of darkness. There were maps, drawings, and a lot of information about unimaginable monsters. Amos was glad that he had brought the book with him.

As he read, Amos learned about the existence of the basilisk. An illustration showed an impressive beast, with a snakelike body and tail, a cock's comb on its head, the beak of a vulture, and rooster-like wings and legs. Described as one of the most abominable and frightening of the world's creatures, this monster was the creation of the magicians of darkness. To create a basilisk, you had to find a rooster's egg that a toad would brood for at least a day. Once it was born, a basilisk could let out a single piercing whistle that was able to paralyze its victim before it attacked.

The basilisk always bit on the tender flesh of the neck. Its bite was extremely venomous and deadly. According to the book, the gaze of a basilisk had the power to wilt vegetation or to roast a bird in flight. So far there was no antidote to the basilisk's bite. No bigger than a chicken at birth, it grew to an imposing size once it took flight. In the air it was as nimble as a snake and as voracious as a vulture. The basilisk killed for the thrill of it. Humans were its prey of choice. The book cited several cities that had been totally decimated by only three or four of these monsters.

Yet this dangerous creature became very vulnerable under certain circumstances. For example, it died instantly if it heard a rooster's *cock-a-doodle-doo*. In addition, just like gorgons, the basilisk was unable see its reflection and survive. So it lived in perpetual fear of mirrors and other reflecting objects that could cause its immediate death.

One by one, the pieces of the puzzle were falling into place in Amos's mind, and he was finally able to imagine a way to free Bratel-la-Grande of the snake-haired women. First, it was obvious that the gorgons would not leave the city without getting back the pendant that was now in Beorf's possession. Second, Yaune the Purifier, who knew of the gorgons' power and therefore should have been able to protect his knights, had made a grave mistake. Since the knights' well-polished armor shined as bright as mirrors, the creatures should have died instantly when facing them—well before they could curse the city. But Yaune had neglected an important fact: gorgons always attacked at night, when mirrors don't reflect anything.

The only way to eliminate these monsters was to install mirrors everywhere and to light hundreds of simultaneous fires in the city. But how did one go about executing such a plan?

Amos wondered. He thought of Beorf's fireflies, but he would never be able to rally thousands, even millions of them.

Deep in thought, Amos was still trying to come up with the best way of eliminating the gorgons when he arrived at a village. He stopped to drink at a fountain.

"Who are you, young man, and what are you doing here?" an old lady asked. She was dressed in white and bent over her cane.

"I'm on my way to the woods of Tarkasis," Amos told her. "Can you point me in the right direction?"

The old lady remained pensive for a moment. "Unfortunately, I can't help you. In two days, you're the second person who's mentioned this forest to me. Isn't it strange?"

Amos was surprised. "Who else asked you about the forest?" he wanted to know.

"A very nice man and his wife. They also inquired if I had seen a boy with long dark hair, wearing leather armor and an earring, and carrying a stick made out of ivory on his back. Yesterday I had not seen him, but today he's right in front of me!"

"Those are my parents!" Amos cried out, deliriously happy to hear news of them. "We had to go our separate ways and I absolutely must find them. Please, madam, tell me which way they went."

"I believe they went that way," she said, pointing.

Amos thanked the old woman, eager to take off. But the woman asked him to stay with her a few more minutes.

"I'm going to tell you something, my young friend," she

said, inviting him to sit down next to her. "I know that you wish to find your parents as soon as possible, but I had a dream last night and I feel I have to tell you about it. I was baking rolls. Every member of my family was around me, and I was doing my best to please them. My children, my grandchildren, my cousins, my nephews, they had all been turned to stone. Then, suddenly, you appeared in my dream. I did not know you and you asked me for something to eat. I gave you three or four rolls. As you bit into one of them, you found a hard-boiled egg. I told you, 'One often finds eggs where they are the least expected.' That's it. I don't believe that dreams are meaningless, so I baked rolls this morning and I brought them with me. I also have some eggs. They're for you and my wish is that you find your parents soon."

Amos thanked her, took the food, and went on his way without really understanding the old woman's dream. When he turned back to wave a last good-bye, the woman had vanished.

The farther Amos walked, the more he thought about what the woman had said: *One often finds eggs where they are the least expected*. He stopped in his tracks. What if the pendant stolen by Yaune all those years ago contained a rooster's egg? That had to be the reason why the magician of darkness wanted so badly to get it back! The pendant itself did not possess any magic or evil power. It was simply the wrapping that protected the egg. The first owner of the pendant had wanted to create a basilisk. It made total sense: this magician commanded an army of gorgons, and wanted to add to his ranks a monster capable of destroying an entire regiment in the blink of an eye.

Amos concluded that the enemy of Bratel-la-Grande exercised power over all living creatures, near or far, who were related to snakes. He had to be malevolent, treacherous, and very dangerous. Beorf was in great danger, and Amos wasn't sure how to warn him.

## —9—

# BEORF, THE GORGONS, AND THE NAGA

The gorgons were in hot pursuit of Beorf. He ran into the forest, his head lowered as he tried to avoid the nighttime obstacles.

The first two days following Amos's departure had been quiet for the humanimal. The gorgons concentrated their search in the city. In his hiding place in the forest, Beorf slept and rested in anticipation of the difficult nights to come. He also pondered at length the best strategy of defense against the invaders. The main idea, simple and efficient, was to get rid of the gorgons one by one.

Beorf perfected dozens of traps and set them everywhere in the forest. He guessed that after several nights spent uselessly searching Bratel-la-Grande, the monsters would inevitably begin to comb the surrounding areas. The gorgons would find various trails—all his own—and would follow them to try to corner any fugitives. The humanimal had purposely left footprints in the fields and in the forest that led directly to the traps.

So as not to be spotted when going from trap to trap, Beorf morphed into a bear. The gorgons were looking for the thief who had stolen the pendant, a human. Not a bear! These creatures would never imagine that the animal and human were one and the same.

One moonlit night, as the gorgons followed Beorf's footprints, three of them encountered quicksand. Hidden from sight, the humanimal saw them disappear into the ground.

"Minus three!" he shouted.

Meanwhile, another small detachment of gorgons found itself in the clearing around his old burned-down house where he kept his beehives. Beorf ordered the bees to attack. The insects swarmed together to form a huge cloud above the gorgons and swooped down on them at full speed. Petrified in flight by the gaze of the monsters, the bees fell from the sky like a torrent of stones and pierced the gorgons' bodies. The insects had sacrificed themselves, allowing Beorf to get rid of five more gorgons.

Soon Beorf noticed that the gorgons' wings enabled them to glide for short distances, but that the snake-haired women were unable to truly fly. He imagined another ambush.

Ditches encircled the tilled fields around the city. These were filled with water through a dike; the water was used to irrigate the farmers' land. Aware of this, Beorf dug several large holes in the fields and covered them with twigs and hay to hide them from view. The following night, eight gorgons fell into the holes. Beorf opened the dike. The water flooded the ditches and holes. All of the gorgons drowned.

Tonight Beorf planned a different snare. He had raided the knights' armory and had planted spears into the ground and hung sabers and swords from tree branches. The only way to avoid these sharp blades was by using a particular path through the branches. Since the gorgons attacked only at night, Beorf had all the time he needed to conceive and set his trap. He trained all afternoon to make sure he knew how to escape the blades. The moment of truth was not far off now.

Beorf could hear the gorgons approaching. He couldn't run fast on two legs. At least his snare wasn't far off. He just had to maintain a good speed to save his life. Out of breath, he took the safe path through the branches. The gorgons, on the other hand, didn't suspect what awaited them and entered the forest of blades at full speed. It was a success! Not one gorgon survived.

Pleased with himself, Beorf returned to his father's library—his main hiding place—to rest for the remainder of the night. He opened the trapdoor, went down the rungs of the ladder, and looked for his lamp of fireflies. Instead, a red light flooded the room.

Seated at his father's desk, a bald man was looking at him. His luminous eyes were a pale yellow, with elongated pupils that dilated and contracted constantly. Scales covered his hands, arms, and neck up to the back of his head. Beorf noticed that the man's eyebrows joined together above his nose, just like his own. The man's nails were horribly long, and a forked tongue came out of his mouth, which was filled with pointed teeth. His bare chest displayed strong muscles, and he wore dozens of gold necklaces adorned with precious gems around his neck. He also wore two large shiny and gilded ear-rings. Legless, his body ended with a very long, gray, snake-like tail covered with black spots.

Beorf tried to flee at the sight of this monstrous being. But as he turned on his heels, he was caught and immobilized by the man's huge snake-tail.

"Ssss, you already want to leave, young friend?" hissed the snake-man. "It's very, ssss, impolite to rush off without letting me, ssss, introduce myself first."

The tail relaxed its stranglehold on Beorf, who turned around to face the hideous intruder. Beorf was shaking.

"Good, ssss, you're a courageous boy, ssss, it's very good. My name is Karmakas, and I traveled far, ssss, to come here. Don't be afraid, young friend, I don't want to, ssss, harm you. Like you, ssss, I am what humans call a humanimal. I would not hurt someone of my own race without good reason. You seem surprised to see me! Ssss, is it the first time that you are in the presence of another member of, ssss, your species?"

Unable to utter a word, Beorf nodded.

"It's very unfortunate, ssss. Do you know why humanimals like us disappeared one after the other? It's because humans hunt us. Humans are, ssss, jealous of our gift, ssss, jealous of our power. Me, I am a naga. Which means in, ssss, ancient parlance, ssss, a snake-man. You are a beorite, a bear-man. You have power over, ssss, bees and some other insects. My power, ssss, is over every crawling, biting, and venomous animal that slithers. I control the gorgons because of their hair. But I have to tell you a secret that, *ssss*, you may already know. I am also a powerful magician."

Beorf took a step back.

"Don't be afraid, I'm a nice, *ssss*, sorcerer. I hurt only, *ssss*, those who hurt me. I turn nasty only, *ssss*, when someone is nasty to me."

With a shaky voice, sweaty hands, and a pounding heart, Beorf interrupted the sorcerer. "Then why did you change all the dwellers of the realm into stone with your army of gorgons? You wanted to get your pendant back and punish Yaune the Purifier, did you not? So it wasn't necessary to injure so many innocent people to satisfy your thirst for vengeance!"

Karmakas laughed. "You are a smart beorite! I think that snake-men are wrong to think that bear-men are the lowest members of the humanimal race. You're not as stupid, *ssss*, as you seem, *ssss*, big fat bear. The inhabitants of this realm were turned to stone because they trusted, *ssss*, a thief and a murderer. I'll tell you my version of the story and you, *ssss*, will understand. I was living peacefully in my hometown, *ssss*, a large city that no longer exists today. In the middle of a stony desert, *ssss*, the nagas and the men who resided in the city lived together in peace. We were craftsmen and our skill, *ssss*, was to work gold. We also had mines and a lot, *ssss*, of wealth. Men grew jealous, *ssss*, of our riches and called on the Knights of Light, *ssss*, to exterminate us and steal our property. Fortunately, the gorgons, *ssss*, came to our rescue, but, *ssss*, too late. My wife and my fifteen children, *ssss*, all of them nagas, were killed by the knights. Yaune the Purifier is the only knight who managed to survive. And do you know why? Because during the final battle against the gorgons, Yaune was, *ssss*, in one of our temples stealing our riches. If he had participated in the battle, he too would be dead, *ssss*, petrified by the gorgons. The pendant belongs to my people and I'm here, *ssss*, to take back what was stolen. That is all, *ssss*. Creatures of my race, those who, *ssss*, survived, wanted to take revenge on men and make them pay for their, *ssss*, avarice and their failure to accept creatures that, *ssss*, do not look like them. Didn't the Knights of Light, *ssss*, kill your father and your mother because they were different?"

Hearing these last words, Beorf began to cry.

"You see, *ssss*, we're alike," the naga went on. "We're both victims of humans and we must join forces, *ssss*, against this powerful enemy. Can you imagine, *ssss*, the bear and the snake united in the humanimals' revenge! Side with me and I will be your new, *ssss*, father."

Having regained some assurance, Beorf looked Karmakas straight in the eyes. "It's true that my parents were killed by humans," he said. "It's also true that humans are sometimes stupid and refuse to accept the things they don't understand. But my father told me many tales about humanimals, and he always said to be wary of snake-men. He claimed that it was because of them, because of their lies and thirst for power, that humans started to persecute humanimals. I had a father and he's dead now. I need no one else to take his place. All you want is to pacify me and gain my trust to get your pendant back. Beorites may not be as intelligent as nagas, but we know to distinguish between good and evil. The pendant is hidden and you'll never get your hands on it!"

The magician clenched his teeth and tightened his muscles. "I'll find a way, *ssss*, to make you talk, you insolent bear." He rose on his huge tail and shouted, "You just signed, *ssss*, your death sentence!"

## —10—

## THE STORYTELLER

An old man was seated on a bench.

"Once upon a time, long ago," he started to tell the children who surrounded him, "there was a young boy named Junos. He lived with his mother in a small cabin in the forest. This boy didn't have the slightest talent for anything. He was a little soft in the head, and his mother didn't know what to do with him. His father had died many years before, and the poor woman had to take care of everything. From the cooking to the washing to working in the fields, she did all she could to ensure her survival and that of her good-for-nothing son. Junos spent his days smelling the flowers, strolling in the fields, and chasing butterflies. One day, as he watched his mother hard at work, he told her, 'Mother, I'm going to town to find a job. With the money I earn, you'll be able to rest.' His mother answered him, 'But, Junos, you're hopeless with your ten fingers, and you always do stupid things.' The boy told her, 'Just wait and see. I'll show you what I can do, Mother.'"

The storyteller had the children's rapt attention. Amos, who was passing by, stopped to hear the end of the story.

"Junos left for the city. He stopped at every farmhouse and at every craftsperson's shop along the way. He asked everyone for work, but each time someone asked him what he was capable of doing, Junos answered honestly, 'I can do nothing.' Of course, upon hearing this, nobody wanted to hire him! At the last farmhouse where he inquired about a job, Junos thought of his mother and how she often reproached him for doing any old thing. When the farmer asked him what he could do, Junos told the truth: 'Sir, I can do any old thing!' He was hired on the spot."

In the small town square, the old man had attracted more and more curious listeners. Several grown-ups were waiting with interest for the end of the tale.

"The whole day, Junos and the farmer spent their time splitting wood and weeding the vegetable garden. In the evening, as a reward for his labor, Junos was given a nice coin. On his way back home, happy with his first day's work, Junos played at tossing the coin in the air and catching it on the fly. A clumsy throw made the coin fall into the stream that ran along the path. Saddened, Junos went home and told his mother of his bad luck.

"She told him, 'Next time, Junos, take what the farmer gives you and put it immediately in your pocket. That way, you won't lose the reward you earned for your work.'

"Junos promised to do what his mother suggested, and the

next day, he went back to the farmhouse. This time he took care of the cows. To thank him for his work, the farmer gave him a bucketful of fresh milk.

"Junos did exactly what his mother had told him to do. He emptied the content of the bucket into his pocket to be sure not to lose it. He was drenched when he reached home. He even had milk in his shoes.

"His mother contained her anger as she listened to his story and told him, 'You must always keep what the farmer gives you in its container, do you understand this, my boy?'

"Junos agreed and the next day, after his day's work, he received a slab of butter. So that the butter would not melt in the sun, the farmer asked Junos for his hat and put the butter inside for protection. The boy put the hat on his head and ran home as fast as he could. The heat of his head melted the butter and it dripped down his hair and face in a yellow mess."

The old storyteller now had a large crowd around him. Everyone seemed to enjoy listening to the tale of this stupid boy. The storyteller was entertaining: he acted out each of the characters and mimicked their expressions. His listeners were enthralled.

"When Junos finished his explanation about the butter, his mother told him, 'You were right to leave the butter in your hat, but you should not have put the hat back on your head! Now take this bag, where you'll put what the farmer gives you. You will carry it on your way home. Do you understand, Junos?' The boy answered that he understood.

"Near the farm where he worked, there was a lovely castle. Junos admired it each time he passed by, and he dreamed of making enough money to be able to live there one day. He also noticed that a young girl always stood on one of the castle's magnificent balconies and that she cried all the time. Junos wondered what made her so sad but he didn't concern himself over it.

"At the end of the next day, the farmer gave him a donkey. Having no need for Junos's services any longer, the farmer gave him this generous gift to thank him for all the work he had done for him. The boy accepted the animal with joy. As recommended by his mother, he tried to put the farmer's gift in the bag, first one of the donkey's front legs, then the other. But he soon realized that the bag was much too small to fit the whole animal in.

"Junos thought of a solution: he put the bag over the donkey's head, squatted, and slipped under the animal. He was going to carry it on his back. He wanted his mother to be proud of him, and for once he was going to do things right. With the bag over his head, the donkey started to struggle and bray. Junos stretched his body up with difficulty, and when he finally managed to lift the animal off the ground, they soon toppled into the dust.

"As Junos tried for a second time to put the animal over his back, he saw a man approach him. It was the king who lived in the nearby castle. He greeted Junos, introduced himself courteously, and confided that his daughter had been crying for years. He had promised her hand to whoever could make her smile. From her balcony, the princess had observed Junos and the donkey. Seeing him struggle with the beast had started her laughing, and now she couldn't stop. And so Junos married the princess, became king, and lived in the castle with his mother. Dear friends, therein lies the proof that to become king, the only requirement is the ability to do nothing or to do any old thing!"

Greeted by thunderous applause, the storyteller saluted his audience and went around with his hat. He received a few coins, and the people who were coming from the market gave him some bread, vegetables, and eggs. He was even handed a sausage. Amos was about to leave when the storyteller called after him.

"You listened to my story, young man, yet you don't give me anything?"

"I regret that I don't have much myself, sir," Amos answered. "I am looking for my parents and I've come from far away. Your story deserves more than my applause, but unfortunately that's all I can offer you."

The old man nodded. "I already have all I need in this hat. The truth is that what I want is company. Would you do me the honor of sharing these provisions with me?"

"With pleasure!" Amos answered. He was starving.

"My name is Junos," said the storyteller, "and you, young man, what is your name?"

Surprised, Amos said, "Is Junos your real name? Like the character in your story?"

"My friend, I take inspiration where I can find it. All my characters, stupid or intelligent, bear my name. This reminds me of the time when my father used to tell me stories. All the heroes of his tales had my name too."

"My name is Amos Daragon and I'm pleased to meet you," Amos said.

"Same here," the old man said. "As you can see, I tell stories for a living, that's all I'm able to do. And I'm always looking for good tales. Tell me where you've come from and what you're doing here. Tell me how you lost your parents too. I'm interested because I lost mine many years ago."

Amos felt that he could trust Junos. There was something youthful and sparkling in the old man's eyes. Except for the old lady in white he had met at the fountain in the neighboring village, Amos had not spoken to anyone in several days. He was happy to find such a likeable person to talk to.

Before he began his story, Amos told the old man that he might not believe everything he was going to hear, yet he swore that it was the pure truth. While savoring the good food that his host offered him, Amos talked about the realm of Omain, about his conversation with the mermaid at the bay of caverns and the task she had entrusted him with. Amos also told him how he had duped Lord Edonf. The young traveler related the events of Bratel-la-Grande and mentioned Barthelemy, now a stone statue like everybody else. Then he described his encounter with Beorf, Yaune the Purifier's game of truth, the blind cat, the druid who had a mushroom growing from his neck, the gorgons, and the book that he had found in Beorf's father's secret library. He told the story of the pendant that he had left with Beorf so that it would not fall into the hands of the gorgons, then he related his departure from Bratel-la-Grande. He expressed his regret at having left his friend behind. He also mentioned what he had learned about the dreadful basilisk.

Amos told Junos everything. But all of it seemed strangely far away now, as if it had happened years ago. By the time he ended his story, night was falling. He and Junos had been talking for more than three hours. Puzzled by this incredible tale, the old man had asked many questions, wanting details about this and that.

"It is a very nice story and I believe every word," Junos said when Amos finished. "Now I'm going to tell you one about the woods of Tarkasis. I hope that you will believe me too. I stopped telling this story several years ago, because everyone thought I was mad. So I decided to conceal the truth and just tell these little made-up stories that children like and that make grown-ups smile. Do you want to hear the story of a great misfortune?"

Happy to be with such an interesting person, Amos was more than willing. "I'm listening, and be assured that I'm ready to believe what you tell me," Amos said.

"Many long years ago," began the old man, "near the woods of Tarkasis, there lived a little boy. He had beautiful dark, curly hair, the big smile of a happy child, an overflowing imagination, and a magnificent dog. He loved this dog more than anything else. His father was a farmer and his mother made the best pancakes in the realm. His parents always told him not to go to the woods. Apparently, there were malevolent forces that made those who dared to venture there disappear. One day the boy's dog was lost, and the boy heard it bark in the forest. He thought that it was in danger and so he entered the forest without taking his parents' warning into account. He walked for a long time. The trees had strange shapes. There were flowers everywhere. It was the most beautiful forest he had ever seen.

"Out of nowhere, a light came out of a flower and started to spin around him. Only many years later did the young boy understand that he had entered the realm of fairies. More lights came to join the first one, and marvelous music started. Imprisoned in a circle of fairies, the child danced and danced and danced with the lights until he dropped to the ground. He fell into a deep sleep under a tree.

"When he woke up, he was fifty years older. His hair had turned white and he had a long beard. He made his way home but the house was no longer here. There was a road now where his father's large garden used to be. His parents, his dog, his house had disappeared.

"He walked on the road and reached a town named Berrion. It's the town we're in today. Totally helpless, he told his story to passersby, claiming that his childhood had been stolen from him. No one wanted to listen to him, and for a long time people thought that he was crazy. Finally, and with difficulty, he accepted his old age and began to tell stories to make a living. This child is still alive and is called Junos, like all the characters of my tales. It is Junos who is talking to you now. It's my own story that I just told you. Could you be the first person to believe me at last?"

Flabbergasted, Amos remembered having heard this story

before. It was the one his father had told him when they were leaving the realm of Omain. Urban claimed to have met this man years ago during his travels with Frilla.

Amos looked at the big tears that ran down the old man's cheeks.

"I believe your story and I make a solemn promise to give you back the childhood that you've searched for all this time," he said. "Take me to the woods of Tarkasis and I'll repair the wrong that was done to you."

# —11—

## THE WOODS OF TARKASIS

Amos spent the night with Junos in the small room the old man rented in a seedy inn. Junos apologized for the lack of comfort that he had to offer his guest. They kept talking for a long while, mostly about fairies, before going to sleep. Junos knew dozens of tales and legends about them.

The old man said that, at the beginning of time, most of the earth had been controlled by the fomors and the firbolgs, who were related to ogres, goblins, and trolls. Later, the fairies arrived from the west; no one knew why or how, probably carried by the ocean wind. They fought the goblins, then the trolls, and finally managed to weaken the ogres enough to force them into exile. These migrated north, to the land of barbarians and ice.

Then, from the east, men arrived. They were powerful warriors, riding big, beautiful horses. They took possession of the land, tilled it and forced the fairies to take refuge in the forest.

Some of the fairies befriended the men, but most stayed in the woods and remained isolated. They found several ways to avoid being disturbed by humans. Their kingdoms were secret and often not accessible. They maintained a strict social hierarchy. Like the bees, the fairies had a queen, workers, and warriors.

However, some men worked together with the creatures of the forest. They were called druids. Their task was to protect nature, especially the animals and the forests—the realms of fairies. It was the fairies that decided which humans were capable of becoming druids. They stole babies from their cribs and replaced them with pieces of magic wood that took the shape of the real infants. Parents never suspected anything. These substitute babies seemed quite normal until they died suddenly, for no apparent reason.

Even today, there is a custom that villagers follow. Although most of them do not believe in supernatural beings, they suspend a pair of open scissors above their children's beds for protection. Since fairies move quickly in the air, the blades will cut them if they try to come close to a crib. Small bells are attached to the clothing of newborn babies, as well as red ribbons and colorful and cumbersome garlands. The jingle of the bells is meant to warn parents if fairies ever try to kidnap a baby. The ribbons and garlands are supposed to hamper their flight.

Amos asked Junos if he knew anything about the tradition of mask wearers. The old man answered that he had heard about a man who had vanquished a dragon all on his own.

The man was nicknamed "the bearer," but the legend did not say anything else.

Worn out, Amos finally fell asleep on the old straw mattress that Junos had placed on the floor. He dreamed of the woman who had given him the rolls and the eggs at the fountain. In his dream, she had become young but still wore her white robe. She kept repeating the same thing to him, "Drive your trident into the stone and open the passage. . . . Drive your trident into the stone and open the passage. . . ."

Amos wanted to find out who this woman was. Why was she speaking to him? he wondered. He also wanted to know about the stone and the meaning of the sentence that she repeated. But he was unable to say a word, and the woman in white vanished. Amos woke up and thought about the strange dream for the rest of the night. When Junos got up in the morning, the two companions ate a little and left for Tarkasis.

After a few hours' walk, Amos and Junos reached the edge of a forest.

"We've arrived," declared the old man. "Yes indeed, it's here that I used to live. Everything has changed, but there are things that can't deceive me. For example, those huge rocks right there are the same. And also this oak tree over here. It was already big before I danced with the fairies. Now it's huge, but it's the same tree. It must be at least twelve years since I've been back. In fact, I've never returned since I emerged from the forest looking like an old man. I was eleven years old."

Junos's recollections made him sad. As for Amos, he was still thinking about his dream from the previous night. There was something so real about it. *Drive your trident into the stone and open the passage*. Amos first looked at the ground to try to find a clue. Then he examined the bark of the trees. He also observed the stones around them.

"Take a good look, Junos; everything here indicates a trail," he said after a long silence. "If you ignore the small shrubs and the ferns and the other small plants, you can see it."

Paying attention to Amos's indications, Junos could make out the semblance of a path through the vegetation.

"What you just discovered is impressive, my friend!" said the old man. "Let's take this trail."

They followed the trail until gigantic conifers and imposing leafy trees blocked their way. In front of them, the path seemed to end. And on the ground, in the high grass, there was a stone. It bore four distinct marks: the first was a simple hole; right under it were three flat holes close to one another; the third mark was elongated; and the fourth looked like a big fissure.

With the old woman's words in mind, Amos grabbed his trident and, in one fluid motion, plunged it into the set of three flat holes. Miraculously, the three teeth of the ivory trident fit the three holes perfectly, just as if it had been made expressly for this purpose.

As the trident entered the stone, the dense and impenetrable forest that faced them opened in a thunder of cracking branches and twisting tree trunks. Doubting their own eyes, Amos and Junos saw a long and dark tunnel take shape in front of them. Amos withdrew his weapon; the door that led to the heart of the woods of Tarkasis was now open. Without a word, the two companions started down the path.

After a few minutes, they arrived at a magnificent clearing overflowing with flowers. On the ground, on the rocks, and on the trees that bordered it, flowers were everywhere. Fairies of different colors and shapes were flying in all directions, absorbed in their work. The sun's rays were blinding, and a brilliant white light inundated the clearing. Seeming to come through the light, a man walked slowly toward them. Amos recognized him. It was the druid he had met in Bratel-la-Grande. He was still dirty and ugly. With the blind cat perched atop his shoulder, he opened his arms.

"Welcome to Gwenfadrille's kingdom, Mr. Daragon. I see that you come with a friend. Let's hurry, the great council of fairies is gathered and impatient to meet you." He looked at Junos and laughed mischievously. "If he wants to, Mr. Junos can accompany you. In fact, I think that he has already met the fairies."

The druid guided Amos and Junos to the center of the woods of Tarkasis. Seven dolmens marked the limits of a gathering space where a multitude of fairies and druids, who had come from near and far, were seated comfortably on large wooden chairs of unusual shapes. They all applauded when Amos appeared. There were small and large fairies; old, hairy druids as well as young beautiful ones; and some strange, small, wrinkled creatures.

Amos and Junos were invited to sit down at the center of the circle. In front of them, two women were wearing crowns: a robust mermaid with light blue hair and a tall fairy with pointed ears. The two creatures were dazzling to look at. They displayed strength and charisma. The pointed-eared fairy, dressed in green, rose to her feet and requested silence with a gesture of her hand.

"Dear friends, I, Gwenfadrille, queen of the woods of Tarkasis, am happy to welcome you to my home for the revival of the tradition of mask wearers.

"The wearer has been chosen by Crivannia, princess of the waters, to accomplish the mission. Our most ancient druid, Mastagane the Muddy, recognized him as such in Bratel-la-Grande, and so did the Lady in White." She pointed to Amos. "Amos Daragon, whom we see here, will become the first mask wearer in a new generation of heroes who will restore stability to this world. If anyone is opposed to his selection, let him or her be heard now or be forever silent!"

The assembled council didn't say a word.

Amos got up. "I'm opposed to this choice!" he said.

A murmur of astonishment rippled through the audience.

"I refuse to serve if I don't understand what is expected of me," Amos went on. "I realize that it's a great honor to be chosen, but I demand to know more about the mission you wish me to undertake, and I want to be told what a mask wearer is."

A perplexed Gwenfadrille looked at Mastagane the Muddy. "Mastagane, did you not tell him?" she asked.

"Yes, a little, but not all," the druid mumbled. "I thought that you would explain in more detail. So I did not completely—"

"Are you saying that this boy came all this way without knowing what a mask wearer is?" interrupted the queen, stretching each of her words out.

"I believe that is so," murmured the druid, looking a little ashamed.

Amos took advantage of the confusion and pulled the white stone out of his pocket.

"I came here first to give you a message, Gwenfadrille," he said. "Your friend Crivannia, princess of the waters, is dead, and her realm has fallen into the hands of the merriens. Before she died, she asked me to bring this white stone to you and tell you that she had chosen me as the mask wearer. But you seem to already know that."

"Yes, we know," admitted the green fairy. "Give me the stone and listen to what I say.

"In ancient times, the world was divided between the sun and the moon, between the creatures of light and the creatures of night. The beings of light represented good, and those of night were the representatives of evil. For centuries, the creatures of the two camps fought deadly battles to ensure the domination on earth of light or of night.

"Tired of these sterile and endless fights, several great kings and queens of both camps decided to meet to try to find a solution. It was necessary to find common ground to restore the peace that everyone wanted. Together they selected humans—the only beings in whom good and evil live jointly—and created the sacred order of the mask wearers. Their task was simple enough: it consisted of working with good and evil, with day and night, to bring balance back into the world. These warriors of equilibrium were given the mission to kill menacing dragons, to calm the ardor of the unicorns, and to reunite the realms that war had divided. These men derived their power from the magic of the elements. Each of them had four masks: that of air, fire, earth, and water. On each of these masks, four power stones were inlaid. Four white stones for air, four blue ones for water, four red ones for fire, and four black ones for earth. Sixteen power stones altogether.

"These warriors succeeded in their mission, and for many years, good and evil existed together in harmony. An eternal peace had been reached, and the mask wearers were not replaced. They discarded their masks and the power stones were shared between the forces of day and night. But recently the night creatures have taken up their arms again. The attack by the merriens against the mermaids is the very proof of that. This is why we wish to revive the order of the mask wearers."

Amos remained silent for a moment, then he asked, "Earlier you mentioned a lady in white. Twice I've seen this woman. Who is she exactly?"

"She is a powerful spirit," explained Gwenfadrille. "She is the conscience that guides the warriors of equilibrium. The Lady in White sponsors each of the mask wearers. She'll protect you and show you the way. Today, if you accept the destiny that we envision for you, I'll give you your first mask—that of air. In it, I'll set the white stone that you brought to me, and the powers of this ancient object will be reborn. You will have to find the three other masks and the fifteen missing stones.

The more masks you possess, the greater your power will be, and the better your control of the elements. Do you accept our offer, Amos?"

Amos thought it over. A deep silence surrounded him. The fairies were holding their breath; they did not move. The druids started to stamp their feet impatiently. And the new princess of the waters, the blue-haired mermaid, was wondering if Crivannia had made the right choice when she selected this boy.

Amos got up again. "I accept, under one condition!" he said.

"This is most unusual," said Gwenfadrille. "But go ahead, we're listening."

"I want the fairies to give back to my friend Junos the childhood they stole from him. I want him to return to his family, where he'll help his father with the vegetable garden, and where he'll eat his mother's delicious pancakes. He must also get his dog back."

Right away, the queen of the fairies answered. "Your request is granted. My fairies will take Junos back to the home of his youth, where he'll find himself exactly at the age he was when he fell under our spell."

Junos burst into tears. "Amos Daragon has kept his promise," he cried with joy. "I'll get my childhood back! I'll see my dog again! And my father! And my mother! Thank you! Thank you, my friend! Thank you with all my heart!"

As he let himself be escorted away by a group of fairies, the old man turned toward Amos.

"I'll pay you back a hundred times for what you just did for me. I swear it on my life, on my soul, and on my parents' heads. See you soon, my friend!"

Very solemnly, Gwenfadrille picked up a magnificent crystal mask that was by her side. It had the shape of a fine-featured man with a bulging forehead. She handed it to Amos and asked him to try it on. The mask adjusted itself perfectly to Amos's face. The fairy then set into it the white power stone sent by Crivannia. Amos got the immediate impression that he was breathing in rhythm with the wind.

"This mask will grow with you," the queen of the fairies declared. "It is your property and your dearest possession. You'll discover its powers on your own. It's not very potent yet, but when the four stones are set into it, you'll have the ability to raise a hurricane and the strength necessary to walk on air. Now let us all pay homage to Amos Daragon and feast in honor of the first human in the second generation of the warriors of equilibrium!"

Everyone present stood up and applauded. Then a joyous music was heard.

## —12—

# BEORF AND MEDUSA

Karmakas had installed himself in the castle at Bratel-la-Grande. With the gorgons' help, he had placed all the villagers—more than one thousand statues—outside the city gates. They were displayed along both sides of the road leading to the capital. The scene was terrifying. Itinerant merchants, travelers, adventurers, and troubadours refused to come close to the city. Everyone who saw the ghastly statues doubled back, vowing never again to set foot in that part of the country.

The gorgons had ransacked the town. Houses were entirely demolished or burned to the ground. A deadly silence had replaced the shouts of children heard in happier days. There was no sign of life—no flowers in bloom and no human activity. Yaune the Purifier's army had been totally defeated. A black flag in the shape of a snake, its mouth open as if ready to strike, flew over the city. The water from the river had been poisoned, the fields were fallow, and the birds had deserted the area.

Karmakas's powerful magic had enabled him to double his army of gorgons. The city was swarming with snakes. Cockroaches, the gorgons' food of choice, crawled over the walls of the castle, into the ruins of houses, and everywhere over the ramparts of Bratel-la-Grande.

For the last three days, Beorf had been buried up to his neck, and had been suffering terrible agonies. He had been blindfolded so that the stare of the gorgons would not petrify him. At night, the monsters often walked over his head and deprived him of sleep. During the day, the sun scorched his face. And every morning, the naga came to visit him. Karmakas was aware of the humanimal's weak spot. He knew that bear-men had unmatched strength and physical endurance. The only thing they could not tolerate was going hungry. So every morning Karmakas tantalized Beorf with bread and honey.

"If you tell me where the pendant is, I'll give you, *ssss*, all the food you want," the sorcerer said. "Tell me where the pendant is and we'll, *ssss*, become a team. I know that, *ssss*, you're hungry. Talk to me, *ssss*, tell me, *ssss*, where my precious pendant is hidden."

Blindfolded, Beorf smelled the fragrance of fresh bread. He imagined the taste of honey on his tongue. His stomach churned with hunger and his whole body begged for food. His taste buds filled his mouth with saliva. Every morning, the torture weakened his will a little more.

"I'll never tell you! I'll die before you get any information out of me," Beorf answered day after day.

Frustrated, the naga always left hissing with rage. Toward the end of the fifth day, Beorf was so exhausted by the pain in his stomach that he wondered if he could hold out any longer.

"Have no fear, I'm here to help you," the voice of a young girl whispered in his ear.

Beorf could feel hands digging around him to remove the dirt. The girl freed him and helped him up.

"I have to warn you that I'm a gorgon. Be very careful never to look into my eyes or you'll straightaway turn into a statue," she warned him. "To make it safer for you, I'm wearing a cloak with a hood that covers my eyes. Now I'll remove your blindfold."

Stunned, Beorf opened his eyes and saw the lower half of the gorgon's face. She was lovely and had a beautiful mouth. Her lips were brown and lush. A few golden-colored snake heads that did not seem to be malicious were sticking out of her hood, moving the fabric gently. Her skin was a pale green.

"Come, we have to flee this place before the sorcerer catches us," she said, extending her hand to him. "Do you know how to get out of this city without going through the main gate?"

"Yes, I know a way," said Beorf. "Follow me!"

Together they made their way to the tunnel that Beorf had dug under one of the city walls. They fled quickly and reached the forest without any problem. Beorf led the young gorgon to a cavern that his parents had always used as a pantry. There, the humanimal plunged headfirst into the food rations, stuffing himself with dried fruit, nuts, honey, grains, and salted meat. Once he was full, Beorf remembered his manners and offered the gorgon something to eat.

"Thank you," said the girl. "I don't eat this kind of food. I only devour insects. I love roaches cooked in toad blood. Delicious! Since you love good food, you should try my recipe sometime."

Beorf felt a little disgusted. His cheeks were pink again and he now felt restored. His body was loosening up after his ordeal, and he was unable to control a noisy, long burp. The young gorgon laughed a crystal-like giggle. Beorf couldn't imagine that this charming creature could be the offspring of such a horrible race. He apologized for his burp.

"Who are you and why did you come to my aid?" he then asked her.

"You would not be able to pronounce my real name," answered the gorgon. "Call me Medusa. That is the name humans often give us. It's a name inherited from Princess Medusa, who was transformed into a hideous woman by a nasty goddess. Many legends exist on the subject of gorgons, but no one really knows the origin of my species. I know that your name is Beorf. It is said that you can morph into a bear. Is that true?"

Flattered that this beautiful young gorgon knew his name, Beorf changed into a bear on the spot.

"True," he said, standing proud and hairy from head to foot.

"Hide your eyes," Medusa said. "I'd like to look at you."

Beorf put a paw over his snout.

Pulling her hood back and uncovering her eyes, Medusa exclaimed, "How magnificent a bear is! I've never seen such an animal. You know, there are only gorgons and snakes where I come from. There are also many stone statues," she added, laughing her enchanting giggle. "To answer your question, I helped you because I too need help. Karmakas is a wicked sorcerer. He controls my kind through his magic, and forced us to come to this realm to do his bidding. If we defy his orders, he tells our snake-hairs to bite our shoulders and backs. It hurts so much that we cry out in pain loud enough to make mountains shake."

She pulled her hood back over her eyes and told Beorf it was safe to look at her.

"We are nocturnal creatures and cannot bear the sun easily," she went on. "This does not mean that we are nasty and cruel. It's true that our power transforms all living creatures that we come across into statues. To avoid such misfortune, my people live in hiding in the arid hills of the east desert. It's the gorgons themselves who sent me to free you.

"I beg you to believe me. We don't want to harm anyone and we know how to bring back to life the stone statues that we create. It's a little complicated, but it can be done. We don't want to wage battle any longer; we only wish to go home and live in peace. But we are unable to fight Karmakas. Our power does not work on him, so we remain his prisoners. The gorgons are his slaves. We must serve him or suffer horrible pain. Look at the skin on my shoulders and you'll understand what I mean."

Medusa pulled down a sleeve of her dress, exposing her shoulder. It was covered with open wounds and scars.

"You see!" she said. "It's difficult for me to believe that my own hair can do this to me."

"Why don't you cut off those nasty beasts, then?"

"Would you cut off your arm or your leg even if it hurt you?" she answered, a little upset. "My hair is a part of me. I love it very much. Each of the golden snakes that you see contains a part of my life. To cut them off would be my death. They're my only friends and my solace. I've known them since I was little, and each one has a name. I feed them and take good care of them."

"May I ask you something?" Beorf asked very politely.

"You may ask whatever you want," Medusa answered.

"I'd love to see your eyes, your entire face."

The gorgon giggled again. "You don't seem to listen to what I tell you, young bear. It's impossible—you'd be instantly turned to stone!"

"I know that it's possible to look at the reflection of a gorgon in a mirror," declared Beorf rather proudly. "I know because I've done it by accident. I have a mirror here and—"

When she heard these words, Medusa panicked. "You have a *mirror*? A mirror! Did you bring me here to kill me? I knew I was wrong to believe in you! I always said to my fellow gorgons that we had to be wary of what looked human. You're vicious and you always wish to kill whatever does not look like you! If you want to kill me, do it now, but stop torturing me by mentioning a mirror!"

Beorf rushed to the mirror that he had noticed a moment earlier among the provisions of food and smashed it on the floor of the cavern. He stomped on it to break it further into pieces.

"There! No more mirror! No more danger! Calm down, please, calm down. I didn't mean to offend or threaten you. I wanted to see your eyes because you are very beautiful. That's all! I swear!"

Medusa calmed down. Beorf saw drops of perspiration running down his friend's neck.

"Always remember, Beorf, that my kind are scared to death of mirrors. A gorgon must never see her reflection in a mirror. She dies immediately, ripped apart completely from the inside, and then she crumbles to dust. It's the worst death that we can imagine. I'd rather cut the snakes off my head one by one than stay in a place where there is a mirror."

Beorf laughed uneasily. "That's fine! I never liked girls who spent their time combing their hair in front of mirrors."

After a moment of silence, and feeling even more ill at ease, he asked, "But tell me, Medusa, there's something I don't understand. I've seen gorgons in the forest and . . . how do I say this? Well, they weren't very pleasant to look at, but you . . ."

The young gorgon started to laugh again. "I see what you mean. When we turn nineteen and a half—the exact age that Medusa was when she was struck by Ceto's curse—our face and body change. We become ugly, just as Medusa did. Some of us escape this curse, but I don't know why. None of the lucky ones has revealed her secret."

"Maybe you'll discover it before you reach that age," Beorf said.

Medusa remained pensive a moment. "You're very sweet, Beorf, do you know that?"

Beorf smiled. "Yes, I know," he said, a little flushed.

## —13—

## THE RETURN TO BERRION

During the feast that the fairies organized for him, Amos ate a lot of dishes he had never tasted before. He drank the nectar of daffodils, daisies, and lilies. He also attended a concert given in his honor, where the tunes he heard were surreal, infinitely pure and delicate. *It's not surprising that Junos was bewitched,* he thought as he remembered his friend's adventure in the forest. Amos went to sleep on the grass as he listened to the celestial music.

In the morning of a new day, the fairies brought him a large glass filled with dew and a piece of cake made of rose petals. Amos then left the forest wearing his mask in which the white stone was set, his ivory trident slung across his shoulder. He took the long path that led in and out of the woods of Tarkasis. When he reached the edge of the forest, he was surprised to see several posted signs that said BY ROYAL EDICT,

THIS FOREST IS FORBIDDEN TO TRESPASSERS. Astonished, he reached the road and observed that it was now paved.

"These things cannot happen in one night!" Amos said to himself.

His surprise was even greater when he arrived at the outskirts of Berrion. The town had grown three times larger. Imposing walls had been erected all around it. A flag was flying over the roof of a newly built castle. A moon and a sun that shared the same circle were displayed on the standard. At the city gate, a guard stopped Amos.

"By royal decree, all children who wish to enter must give their names!" the guard said.

Amos was truly bewildered. The last time he had been here, there had been no army. And certainly no knights dressed in magnificent armor and equipped with long swords! How could things have changed so much in only one night? Then Amos remembered that Junos, who had been bewitched by the fairies, had danced for almost fifty years in the woods of Tarkasis. Yet Amos was still twelve years old, not an old man. So he had not been subjected to the same spell as Junos. He hadn't changed, but the world around him had.

"My name is Amos Daragon," he answered timidly.

"Repeat your name, young man," the guard insisted.

"Amos . . . Amos Daragon."

"If that is indeed your name, you must follow me immediately."

Amos didn't protest. He followed the guard into the city

and up to the castle. Everything he saw around him—the houses, inns, shops, marketplace, streets, people—everything was different. The day before, he had left a village where the inhabitants had a hard time making a living. Today he was walking the streets of a large and fortified city where everyone seemed to enjoy a prosperous lifestyle. Amos was puzzled.

When they reached the castle, the guard took him to a vast room where a throne stood. Amos remained there alone for a while, then, suddenly, the large doors of the room opened. A middle-aged man ran toward him and lifted him from the ground.

"Amos! My friend! You're back! How are you?" the man cried out. "I've been waiting for you a long time! This is a great day! It's such a pleasure to see you again!"

Finally the man put him down. Amos could not believe it. It was Junos who stood in front of him! He was a good ten years younger than when he had last seen him, and he beamed with pleasure as he looked at his friend again.

"Excuse me, Junos," Amos said. "But could you explain what's going on? Yesterday you got your childhood back and now you're older again. Did you see your parents? Did you find your dog? What is happening? You were a storyteller and now you're a king? I don't understand."

Junos smiled. "Sit down on my throne and I'll explain."

Amos did as he was told. "But if you're a king now, Junos," he said, "it's either because you can do nothing or you got used to doing any old thing!"

Junos's laughter filled the large room. "My story! You

remember it? It has been years since I told it. I'm not sure that I could even tell it anymore!"

"First, explain to me what's going on, Junos, then I'll refresh your memory. I heard your tale from your own mouth two days ago, and you looked like an old man then. Now you're a man in the prime of your life."

Junos caught his breath and began:

"I'll do as I did in former times when I told stories to survive. I was older and uglier than I am today, but . . . Let me get started. Once upon a time, there was a young boy who ventured into the woods of Tarkasis to retrieve his dog. He danced with the fairies that lived there and he suddenly grew old. He spent twelve years telling stories to make enough money to eat; he met Amos Daragon, who became his friend, and thanks to him, he got his youth back. So far it's a familiar story. You know the beginning but not the end." He looked at Amos, who nodded. "What follows is better.

"So the boy, who had fifty years of life stolen from him, was young once more. He took a five-decade leap back! He found himself in the same forest, exactly one hour after his first encounter with the fairies. He found his dog and his parents. No one ever knew that he had lived so many years as a miserable old man. But while the young boy got his young body back, he kept his adult memory. Since Junos had a debt to repay his best friend, who in fact was not even born yet, he chose to become a knight and went to a nearby kingdom to learn the art of warfare. After many years of faithful service, the king asked Junos—now his best knight—what it was he wanted more than anything else. Junos requested and was granted the land of Berrion. He had a large city built there. He formed an army, created the order of the Knights of Equilibrium, and waited for the day he would greet his good friend Amos Daragon when he stepped out of the forest. He also had signs put up near the woods of Tarkasis so that anyone who ventured there would steer clear of the forest and let the fairies live in peace."

"Amazing!" Amos exclaimed. "So you've been waiting fifty years for me to come out of the forest?"

"Yes, Amos. I've been waiting fifty years for you," Junos, lord and master of Berrion, said. "You gave me back my youth. Thanks to you, I had a happy childhood and my parents died in my arms, proud of what I had become. Thanks to you, I found my beloved dog and spoiled it its whole life long. Thanks to you, I even had time to learn how to cook! With my mother's recipe, I'm the best pancake maker in the realm. I still remember the council of the great fairies that I attended. I know about your mission and the task expected of you. I also remember that a very long time ago, at least for me, you told me that Bratel-la-Grande had fallen into the gorgons' hands. I sent my men there and they confirmed this fact. I created the order of the Knights of Equilibrium to serve you and help you in your mission. An army of four hundred men awaits your orders, dear mask wearer!"

Amos was speechless. Everything was happening so fast.

"By the way," Junos went on, tears in his eyes, "I also asked my men to search all the lands of Berrion, and we found your parents. They're in one of the rooms of the castle. Come, let us go see them!"

ᴪ

The reunion was very moving. Amos threw himself into his parents' arms and they in turn jumped with joy. Urban explained to Amos how he and Frilla had barely had time to flee Bratel-la-Grande. Immediately after Amos and Beorf were banished, they had devised a plan. They packed their belongings and loaded them onto a horse. Since they knew where Barthelemy kept his armor, Urban slipped it on. At the door of the city, riding his mount proudly, he presented himself as a knight. Walking by the side of the horse, her hands tied behind her back, Frilla pretended to be a prisoner. Urban gave the order to open the gates of the city once more to expel the mother of one of the two boys banished earlier. The guard obeyed. As soon as the gates closed behind them, Frilla got rid of the rope and jumped on the horse, and she and Urban sped off into the night. That was how they had managed to escape before the gorgons' attack.

In turn, Amos wanted to tell his parents *his* story, but Junos had already related to Urban and Frilla how he had met their son, and told them of their journey into the woods of Tarkasis.

That night, before going to bed in the room Junos had chosen for him, Amos tried on the mask again. He was alone, and the moment seemed propitious to test his new skill. For the first time, he noticed that the mask disappeared completely when it touched his skin. Looking at his reflection in the mirror, Amos was surprised to realize that although he could feel the mask move over his face, it remained invisible to the human eye. Amos confirmed this when he opened the door of his room and asked a guard posted in the corridor to come inside and open a window that was stuck. The man obliged, oblivious to the mask Amos still wore.

Once the guard left, Amos grew dizzy. He was breathing as he had never done before. It was as if the air were entering every pore of his skin. He lifted his head and saw the Lady in White. She was now eight years old and was playing with the pillows on the bed.

"Do not worry," she said casually. "The mask molds to your features. It will take a bit of time before it knows you. Right now it is probing you and soon it will be in touch with your mind. Then it will send a spark."

As the Lady in White had warned, Amos suddenly felt as if a bolt of lightning were shooting through his body. He cried out. The pain in his head was so intense that he fell to his knees, paralyzed by the throbbing that kept getting worse. It felt like torture. After a few agonizing minutes, the pain disappeared and Amos was able to get to his feet again. The little girl in her white dress was jumping up and down on the bed now.

"That's it! You'll never be able to remove this mask from your face," she told him. "The other masks, should you find them, will fit together over this one. The power of the wind is now in you! This force will return to the mask only when you die. Come, now!"

The Lady in White took Amos by the hand and led him toward the balcony. From there, they had a splendid view of the city of Berrion. Night had fallen. Torches and bonfires illuminated the nocturnal activities.

"Go ahead," she said. "Raise the wind!"

Amos extended his left arm. A strong and steady breeze made the torches flicker over a large part of the city.

"Since you are now endowed with a great gift, I believe that you no longer need me," the little girl in white said. "You'll come to realize that you can also move a large quantity of air if you blow through your mouth. And your trident, or any other throwable weapon, will be able to cover very long distances. You'll also be able to talk and have your words travel miles from where you are. Birds are now your friends. Don't abuse their trust!"

The girl ran toward the bed, pulled up the blankets, slipped under the sheets, and instantly vanished. Once more, Amos had been unable to say a word.

Ψ

Amos opened his eyes and sat up quickly. He was in bed. It was morning. He couldn't feel the mask on his face. He looked around him. The mask had disappeared. He looked in the mirror: nothing on his face. He got up and approached a gray-tufted titmouse that was sunbathing on the balcony. The bird did not seem the least bit frightened. Amos extended his hand and asked softly if it would mind coming to rest on his arm. Right away the titmouse left the balcony railing and landed on his hand.

"It's true, then," Amos mused out loud. "All I went through last night is true. It wasn't a dream. The mask has fit itself onto my face and I possess all its powers. And to think that only one of the four stones is set into it!"

A crow flew by. The bird nodded to Amos and continued on its way. Amos leaned on the rail of the balcony.

*It's difficult to imagine what my strength will be when the three other stones are there*, he thought. *And there are three other masks to find. I hope I'll be able to gather them in my lifetime and accomplish what is expected of me*.

In the small square below, children were trying in vain to fly a kite. Amos concentrated and lifted his left hand until the wind carried the kite high into the sky. The children shouted with joy. After a few minutes, the young mask wearer lost his concentration and the kite tumbled onto the nose of a passerby. Dizzy, Amos fell to the ground and the titmouse flew off.

*The magic of the elements is exhausting*, he thought. *You need total and uninterrupted focus to sustain any effort. If what happened last night was not a dream, I must try one last thing this morning*.

With both hands, Amos gathered air just as one collects snow. He made a transparent ball out of it, put it over his mouth, and whispered a message into it.

"Beorf, it's Amos. I am well and I will come as soon as possible with an army of four hundred knights. Hold tight, my friend, I will soon be at your side."

Amos saw the words twirl in the ball, unable to escape. Then, with all his strength, he hurled the ball.

"Go close to the ear of my friend Beorf Bromanson and shatter!" he instructed loudly.

He looked on as the ball flew in the direction of Bratel-la-Grande, where he hoped that his friend was still alive. He missed Beorf and regretted having left him behind. Lost in thought, Amos went down to the dining hall of the castle to nibble on something. Junos was there, helping the servants clean the tables after the knights' breakfast.

"I've asked my men to get ready so we can leave soon," Junos told Amos. "We have a long road ahead and many dangers await us. We have to be well rested if we hope to take Bratel-la-Grande back from the evil forces that occupy it. We can discuss our strategy later on. Long live the Knights of Equilibrium!"

As Amos looked at Junos, he felt dizzy again and lost consciousness. His last act of magic had drained him of all his energy.

# —14—

## THE EYES OF MEDUSA

For the last three days, Beorf and Medusa had shared the same hiding place. They did not go out of the cavern even once. Inside the pantry were enough provisions to allow them to survive for several weeks. The young gorgon had to be content with the few insects she found there. She did not like this diet too much. She would have preferred roaches rather than spiders.

Violent thunderstorms and heavy rains kept them confined, but gave them the chance to talk at length. Beorf told Medusa about his life in the forest, his daily routine with his parents, and his games with the bees. The more time he spent with her, the more he liked Medusa. Never before had he had the occasion to make friends, and meeting her had filled his heart with unknown happiness. The young gorgon was sweet and attentive, calm and easygoing.

Out of straw and small pieces of wood, Beorf made a

charming doll in Medusa's image. The young gorgon kissed him tenderly on the cheek to thank him. Beorf wished that their time in the cavern would never end. He felt respected and liked. He had fallen in love very fast. Medusa's words sounded like soft music to his ears. At night they slept back-to-back to keep warm. The fat boy lived in a constant state of happiness. Hours seemed like minutes; days like hours.

On the morning of the fourth day, Medusa asked Beorf if he knew why the sorcerer had taken such an interest in Bratel-la-Grande.

"Oh, yes, I do know," Beorf answered as he stuffed himself with hazelnuts. "He's looking for a pendant. But don't worry, he'll never find it!"

"Why?" asked the gorgon, surprised by Beorf's confident tone.

"Because I hid it myself," Beorf answered proudly. "I don't know what this pendant represents for the snake-man or what power it has. He told me a story about it, but I didn't believe a word of what he said. One has to be wary of nagas. They're wily liars."

Medusa thought for a moment. "But if we had the pendant, maybe we could use it against him," she said. "I know a little bit about magic. If I could see it, it might help us understand its power."

"I believe it's more dangerous to have it in our hands than to leave it where it's hidden. I think that Karmakas could detect its presence. He would be after us in no time."

"Yes, you're right, my friend," Medusa answered. "Yet I'm curious to know where it's hidden."

"I'd like to tell you but I won't. If Karmakas ever captured you, you'd be tortured until he got the secret."

Vexed, the young gorgon turned her back to him. "If Karmakas were to capture me, I'd be killed right away for having helped you to escape," she said. "I understand that you wish to keep the hiding place secret. But I thought I was your friend. Back home, we tell everything to our friends. You may be right not to trust me. After all, I'm only a vicious gorgon!"

"Of course you're my friend. Even my best friend," Beorf said. He was confused. "It's to protect you that I don't want to tell you where the pendant is."

"Pardon me," Medusa said after a while. "I know that you're doing this for my own good. I'm too inquisitive. I admire you so much! I'd just like to know what trick you used to keep the sorcerer from finding his pendant, that's all."

Beorf was touched by the compliment. "All right, I'll tell you. It will be our secret," he said, coming close to her ear. "I hid the pendant before I met Karmakas. My friend Amos Daragon told me that something or someone very powerful was looking for it. After he left for the woods of Tarkasis, I thought of a spot where no one would look for it. The pendant is hidden in Bratel-la-Grande's cemetery. There are thousands of tombs and dozens of vaults there. It's like a labyrinth of hiding places. I thought the gorgons would never question the dead, and I was right. I'm sure that Karmakas will never think to search there, either."

Medusa smiled tenderly. "Thank you for trusting me, my friend. I'll never tell this secret to anyone. But if I may ask you one more question, where did you hide it in the cemetery?"

"I'd rather keep that to myself," Beorf answered. "It's difficult to explain to someone who doesn't know the place. I went there with my bees because the cemetery is covered with beautiful flowers rich in pollen. If you want, I'll take you there later."

At that precise moment, Karmakas entered the cavern. His long tail was gone and he moved on two legs. Promptly he grabbed Medusa and put a dagger to her throat.

"*Ssss*, it was about time! I've been watching you, *ssss*, for three days. I was becoming *ssss*, impatient. Now, young beorite, *ssss*, you will go to the cemetery and, *ssss*, bring me back my pendant. If not, *ssss*, I'll kill your friend. One less gorgon makes no difference to my army."

Medusa seemed calm in spite of the menacing blade touching her throat.

"Don't yield to this blackmail, Beorf, don't tell him anything!" she said. "If you save me, you will imperil many other people! Let him kill me! He'll kill us anyway once he gets the pendant. Save your life and keep quiet!"

Beorf did not know what to do.

"Decide quickly!" Karmakas said, pushing the blade against the skin of the young gorgon.

Medusa howled in pain.

Unable to see his friend suffer, Beorf shouted, "All right, let her live and I'll give you the pendant. Swear that you won't hurt her!"

"I swear," the naga answered. "I'll wait for you here, *ssss*, with her, *ssss*, to be sure that you come back. Retrieve my, *ssss*, pendant and hurry. My patience is running, *ssss*, thin."

Beorf morphed into his bear form and left the cavern in one leap. He ran as fast as he could to Bratel-la-Grande's cemetery. On his way, he tried to come up with a solution, a way to outsmart the sorcerer. *If only Amos were here!* he thought. *He would find a way to keep the pendant* and *save Medusa.* One thing was clear to him: the gorgon had to be saved, and he would do all he could to keep her alive—and close to him. He was ready to sacrifice his own life to rescue her.

Once in the cemetery, Beorf approached a vault belonging to a prominent family in the city. He moved one of the stones that had become loose over the years and recovered the pendant quickly. The beorite breathed a little easier with the precious object between his paws. His thoughts were confused and his fear of losing Medusa was torturing him. He was trapped! There was no reason for the naga to spare their lives once he got the pendant back. Beorf had done everything he could to keep the pendant from falling into the sorcerer's hands. Now he had no choice: he had to face death with dignity, hoping for Karmakas's mercy. With these somber thoughts, he walked back holding the pendant between his teeth.

When he reached the cavern, Beorf took his human form again. He was perspiring.

"Here is your pendant!" he told the sorcerer, who was still threatening Medusa with his weapon. "Now, spare us. If you really have to kill someone to satisfy your anger, take my life, but let Medusa live. She has nothing to do with this. It's between you and me!"

Karmakas grabbed the pendant. He let out a monstrous

laugh. "Very well, *ssss*, I will take your life and, *ssss*, let Medusa live. You agree, *ssss*, to this?"

Resigned, Beorf took a deep breath. "Yes, my life for hers!" he said solemnly.

The naga seemed to enjoy Beorf's predicament. He put his dagger aside and removed the hood from Medusa's head.

"You see, *ssss*, my beautiful child," he said, addressing the young gorgon whose back faced Beorf, "how, *ssss*, everything ends well for you!"

Medusa hugged Karmakas and kissed his cheek.

"You told me once that beorites were stupid and sentimental," she said. "You were right! It was easy to make him talk. So easy. Thank you for believing in me, Father. I think I played my part rather well."

Beorf stared at them openmouthed. He could not believe his ears or his eyes. Karmakas looked at him smugly.

"Let me introduce my, *ssss*, daughter Medusa," he said. "Every gorgon is, *ssss*, my child. We are, *ssss*, a large family!"

Medusa brought her hood down over her eyes and turned toward Beorf.

"Did you really believe that you had become my friend?" she said to him. "I hate hairy creatures. They disgust me! You stink like a wild beast and I find you repulsive. I don't like you. In fact, I hate you. If you used your mind more often than your stomach, you'd have understood that I was not sincere. It was so simple to make you believe that I was your friend. I don't deserve my father's praise. You are stupid, Beorf!"

Beorf held back tears. "I really loved you, Medusa," he said. "And even if I know now that you lied and that I'm going to die, I'll never regret the time I spent with you. They were the best moments of my life."

"Be quiet!" cried the gorgon. "You're pitiful. But I will do something for you. In exchange for the stupid doll that you made me, I'll grant one of your wishes. I'll let you see my eyes. They will be the last thing you see before turning to stone. It would be a pity to deprive you of them!"

Beorf's desire to see Medusa's eyes was so strong that when she pulled up her hood, Beorf did not even think of turning his head away. He saw that her eyes were bloodred. At the center of each pupil a light flickered like a blazing fire. He was suddenly unable to move. He felt his skin harden. A wave of cold invaded his body. But just before he turned to stone, Beorf spoke.

"You have the most beautiful eyes in the world, Medusa," he said tenderly.

# —15—

## THE NEW MISSION

For almost a week, Medusa had returned every day to the cavern where Beorf stood petrified and lifeless. She studied his honest face, now frozen in stone. The gorgon could not get his last words out of her mind: *You have the most beautiful eyes in the world, Medusa*. Right until the end, Beorf had not wavered. He had proven that his feelings for her were true.

Medusa did not understand his behavior. Love did not exist among gorgons. It was a feeling to be avoided, a weakness attributed to other races. Love and friendship were ridiculed. Having real friends was unheard of in Medusa's country. It was only to survive that the weakest united with the strongest ones. At home, daily life was a constant struggle to gain power, to lead clans, to find food, and to secure a place to sleep.

Since her childhood, Medusa had known only the cruelty of her fellow gorgons. The only being who had given her something similar to affection was her father. Karmakas took in the weakest gorgons and looked after them. From then on, they had to serve him without balking. This was the way he had created a powerful army. Each gorgon knew his power and nobody dared to defy him. He wanted to be called Father and promoted his best soldiers. All the highest-ranking gorgons were called Mother. The magician had thus managed to create a false sense of family.

Beorf had told Medusa a lot about his own parents, but she had been unable to understand that sort of relationship. At home, there were no males. Gorgons were all women. Legend said that the first gorgon—the gorgon who had been transformed by Ceto—reproduced herself each time a drop of her blood fell on the ground. In fact, gorgons reproduced by means of their hair. A new gorgon was born out of each snake-hair. After reaching maturity, the reptile fell on the ground and in time became a gorgon. Therefore, Medusa had never known a close family structure. It was each gorgon for herself. To help the youngest ones, or to take care of the eldest, was out of the question. Life was difficult, and only the strongest, most cunning, and most vicious managed to survive.

Medusa had not lied to Beorf when she told him that Karmakas was in control of her snake-hairs through his magic. When a gorgon did not obey the sorcerer's orders, the reptiles bit the gorgon's face and shoulders pitilessly. The pain was so intense that it destroyed any desire for revolt or independence.

When Karmakas had realized that the humanimal refused to talk in spite of his hunger, he had decided to ensnare him.

Karmakas ordered Medusa to free Beorf and make him believe that she was his friend. He then listened to every conversation that the gorgon and man-bear had in the cavern through the intermediary of the golden snakes of the gorgon's hair. The heart of a beorite was as big as its stomach. The sorcerer's ruse had proven successful.

Now Karmakas had the pendant, and he remained locked inside Bratel-la-Grande's castle. He had decreed that no one was to leave the capital. But Medusa knew Beorf's secret passage and refused to obey the sorcerer. Every day, she slipped out of the city through the secret tunnel and went to be with the young humanimal.

There was something fascinating about this boy. Looking at him, the young gorgon felt a new feeling grow inside of her—a sense of emptiness that she had never known before. She wanted to take him in her arms, to watch him stuff himself with nuts, to listen to his chatter, and to feel the warmth of his back against hers. The feeling that was growing slowly within her gave her increasing pain. It wasn't like the pain from a snakebite or a wound received in battle. It was more acute, deeper and more serious.

With her hand, she caressed Beorf's stone face as she remembered his good humor and innocence. He would never again be alive by her side. To break a gorgon's spell, the gorgon had to be killed by seeing her own reflection. This was the only way to bring a stone statue back to life, the only way to reverse the curse. She would never see Beorf alive again. For the first time ever, she missed someone. She caught herself laughing at the thought of Beorf's silliness and cried to see him prisoner of her curse. She had betrayed her only friend and felt horribly guilty.

As she caressed Beorf's face one last time before going back to Bratel-la-Grande, a puff of wind entered the cavern. It went around the space carefully, brushing each object, whirling against the cavern walls. It seemed to be looking for something. The wind surrounded Medusa, then Beorf. It gathered in front of Beorf's face, forming a translucent sphere that tried to enter into Beorf's ears but could not penetrate the stone. Unable to deliver its message, the sphere broke in pieces and Medusa heard a boy's voice.

"Beorf, it's me, Amos. I am well and will come as soon as possible with an army of four hundred knights. Hold tight, I'll be there soon."

Medusa remembered that Beorf had mentioned that his friend Amos Daragon had left to go to the woods of Tarkasis. But he had never said that Amos was so powerful. Now Amos was coming with an army to take back Bratel-la-Grande. The young gorgon left the cavern in a hurry to go and warn Karmakas. Midway, she changed her mind.

*If I tell the sorcerer,* she thought, *I'll betray Beorf a second time. But if I keep quiet, the knights will launch a surprise attack and take back the city. My fellow gorgons will be destroyed. I might lose my life too.*

Faced with this dilemma, Medusa sat down to think. She did not want to hurt anyone again. Her heart had discovered the importance of friendship. The fate of humans and that of gorgons was in her hands. She had to make a decision and take a side once and for all. She hurried back to the cavern.

As she stood in front of Beorf, she looked at him from head to toe.

"You too have the most beautiful eyes, my friend," she whispered.

Once he had the skull pendant in his hands, Karmakas had rushed to the castle of Bratel-la-Grande. Installed in his new quarters, he had told his gorgon servants that he was on no account to be disturbed. The naga spent hours at a time looking at the pendant. He fondled it between his long fingers, smiling with contentment. At last the sorcerer had gotten his property back. After he had searched so many years for Yaune the Purifier, his efforts had been fully rewarded. His enemies, the Knights of Light, were now just harmless statues. He would be able to give life to his basilisk.

Karmakas felt a renewed strength, a courage fueled by a desire for revenge. He was going to create a living weapon capable of destroying humans, a weapon that would assure his reign on earth. He would start by extending his power from city to city, from realm to realm, and then take control of all of this part of the world. His armies of gorgons would go north to attack barbarians, then south to seize the rich and prosperous countries located on the other side of the ocean. Nothing could derail his plan. The gods of darkness would thank him and grant him infinite power. He might even be elevated to the rank of demigod!

Karmakas came from a faraway country close to Hyperborea, where humanimals like him were considered devils. He lived in a large city cut into the stone face of arid mountains. From an early age, he had shown a special talent for magic. He knew better than anyone else how to control snakes. Having noticed this gift, his parents had entrusted him to a sect that worshipped Seth—a snake-headed god. Karmakas became a powerful sorcerer, quickly outshining his teachers. He easily inspired respect and fear.

As soon as he had been proclaimed king and master of the city, Karmakas had encouraged the dwellers to revolt against humans. His arrogance and his unbridled ambition had driven him to wage a merciless war against all the surrounding kingdoms. Hordes of snake-men had attacked and ransacked cities and villages, leaving only misery and desolation in their wake. Tired of these incessant wars, several humanimals of his own species had decided to get rid of him. They wanted another leader. Karmakas didn't care. He used his powers to form an army of gorgons that he led against his own people. To punish them for their treason, he had all the inhabitants killed. The snake-headed god, Seth, took notice and appeared to him; he offered Karmakas a rooster's egg.

The sorcerer never had time to create his basilisk. The Knights of Light had been called to help the humans fight against evil and Karmakas. He had hidden his precious egg in the pendant that Yaune the Purifier managed to steal. During the battle, a spear went through Karmakas's body. He hovered between life and death for several months and had to rest for many long years before recovering his strength and his powers. Then he began his search for Yaune the Purifier and for the pendant. Now his search was over. He was finally going to create a basilisk that could single-handedly destroy entire armies and cities.

For several days Karmakas spent time alone in his castle, looking at and caressing the pendant. He had gotten it back physically, but he needed to repossess it mentally—to reinvest it with his power. When he felt ready, the sorcerer went to his bedroom. He opened the lid of a gold box and took out a black vial. Two diamond snake fangs decorated the vial's cork. The sorcerer lifted the vial toward the sky and pronounced some magic words. Then he uncorked the vial and drank some of the liquid. Right away he lost consciousness and fell to the ground, hitting his head. The sorcerer felt his soul leave his body.

Karmakas was now walking along a corridor with grimy walls. He reached a temple built entirely of human bones. The columns that supported the roof were made of skulls. Tibia and femur bones were set into the walls, creating a morbid and frightening mosaic. In the center of the temple, a snake-headed man sat on a golden throne. His skin was light red in color and his hands resembled strong eagle talons.

"Your servant, *ssss*, is here, powerful Seth," Karmakas said as he kneeled in front of Seth, the god of jealousy and treachery. "I bring you, *ssss*, some good news. Are you willing to listen?"

The god blinked twice in agreement.

"I've recaptured the pendant that, *ssss*, contains the rooster egg. In a day, I'll possess a basilisk, *ssss*, to lead my army of gorgons. No human or any other creature of light, *ssss*, will be able to resist."

Seth seemed delighted. "Very well! The war has begun," he said. "All the gods of evil are united and ready to seize the world. Our creatures of water are already winning many aquatic kingdoms. We rely on you, Karmakas, to extend the force of darkness over earth. You're one of our most faithful servants and we hold you in much esteem. Be careful, however. Remember the long tradition of the mask wearers. The Lady in White has revived this force that has been extinct for generations. A young warrior of equilibrium has been chosen. He will visit you soon. He's not very experienced and so possesses little power. Eliminate him quickly, as well as his accompanying army."

Karmakas got up, bowed to his master, and left the sinister temple. He took the corridor, returned to his body, and then woke up abruptly. Tired by his journey, the naga went to his laboratory in the depths of the castle. A lot of potions and flasks filled with poison were there, as well as a big black book. He grabbed the pendant, broke it between his strong fingers, and took out the rooster egg. Much smaller than the egg of a hen, it was pale green with gray spots; its shell was as hard as stone. Karmakas put it in a wooden box that he had made himself and sat a big toad on top of it. The toad covered the egg with its huge body. The magician closed the lid of the box, which was pierced with holes that allowed the toad to breathe.

Karmakas then went up to the main room of the castle and requested that Medusa be brought to him. A few minutes later, the young gorgon came in.

"You called for me, Father?" she asked.

"Yes," said Karmakas. "Listen to me carefully, *ssss*. I've another mission for you, *ssss*, of the highest importance. I know that, *ssss*, an army will arrive here soon, *ssss*, to take back the city. You'll go, *ssss*, to meet and intercept it. Among the soldiers, there'll be a human, *ssss*, who has the title of mask wearer. You must, *ssss*, gain his trust and, *ssss*, turn him into stone later. Once he's petrified, *ssss*, I'll send hordes of snakes to destroy his army. The gorgons, *ssss*, will take care of the survivors. Go forth and do not come back, *ssss*, until your mission is accomplished."

Medusa could not believe her ears. She had barely heard Amos's message in the cavern and Karmakas already knew of it! How had he found out so quickly that an army was coming? The sorcerer was powerful; she knew she had better obey him if she wanted to stay alive. The fear that the naga—her father—inspired made her tremble. It took all her self-control to keep her composure.

"I'll do my best to please you," she answered.

"Leave now; I've, *ssss*, other things to do," Karmakas commanded.

Then, lost in thought, the naga added softly to himself, "My basilisk, *ssss*, is waiting for me."

## —16—

## THE BERRION ARMY

For four days, the Knights of Equilibrium prepared to follow Amos's recommendations. Shields were polished until they reflected everything in front of them like mirrors. They had to shine at all times. The blacksmiths of Berrion had done their work perfectly. The large shields of the infantry shone in the sun, and so did the round ones used by the archers.

Thanks to a meticulous reading of the book *Al-Qatrum, the Territories of Darkness*, Amos established a war strategy. He requested that two mongooses be captured for every one of his knights. The animals would protect them against a possible snake attack. The Lady in White had appeared to him, warning him against an eventual downpour of vipers that the enemy could launch with their magic power. Men combed the land of Berrion and that of surrounding kingdoms, and seven hundred and seventy-seven mongooses were caught and distributed among the four hundred knights who formed the Berrion army. The knights were ordered not to feed the animals during their journey to Bratel-la-Grande. It was vital that the snake eaters be famished at the time of their confrontation with the reptiles.

Amos chose a rooster with the most piercing crow among the roosters of Berrion. Because of the mask wearer's power over birds, the rooster followed him everywhere.

As for Junos, he directed his troops with jubilation. He relied completely on Amos's intelligence, obeying the boy without question. The king of Berrion even hired a bard, who sang and played many instruments to encourage the brave soldiers.

In this festive mood, Amos and the army left the city of Berrion to liberate Bratel-la-Grande from the dreaded gorgons. When the dwellers in each of the villages they passed saw the flag of the Knights of Equilibrium flapping in the wind, they welcomed them with thunderous applause. All had heard of their mission and wanted to salute these men who had become heroes and seemed indestructible.

Urban and Frilla were not warriors, so their presence on the field would have served no purpose. They stayed in Berrion to await their son's return. They trusted Amos and left him free to choose his own destiny.

For five long days, the horses galloped from sunrise to sunset. At the end of the fifth day, the soldiers reached the border of the Knights of Light's realm, and scouts were sent to Bratel-la-Grande. On each side of the road leading to the capital, hundreds of statues were aligned as a macabre guard of honor. It was easy to guess that all the men, women, children, and animals of the city had been turned to stone.

When the scouts returned, trembling and chattering about what they had seen, the rest of the army started to lose its enthusiasm and confidence. The knights were faced with a fierce enemy capable of impressive feats. Amos and Junos conferred and decided that it was too late in the day for the army to go any farther. They set up camp and men were assigned to guard duty.

In vain Junos tried to raise his men's morale. Most of them had little combat experience and felt powerless in front of such danger. The bard no longer sang, and begged his master to let him go home. As the sun was setting on the horizon, Amos and Junos sat around a bonfire, discussing the best strategy to retake Bratel-la-Grande.

A guard rushed over and interrupted them. "There is a very strange girl who wants to talk to you, Master Daragon," he said. "Shall I bring her here or send her away?"

Puzzled, Amos wanted to see this unexpected visitor. She was brought to him, escorted by four knights. She wore a cloak with a large hood that covered her eyes. Amos noticed with alarm that small golden snakes were wriggling in the opening of her hood. A few steps away from him, the mongooses began to fidget nervously in their cages. Even before the girl realized who he was, Amos turned abruptly toward Junos and said, "It's a gorgon!"

Right away the king shouted at the top of his voice, *"Guards! Raise the mirror-shields! A gorgon has entered the camp!"*

Within seconds, the girl was surrounded by mirrors. She threw herself to the ground, her face cast downward.

"Please," she implored, shaking from head to toe, "don't hurt me! My name is Medusa. I come alone and I am here as a friend! Please don't hurt me! Tell Amos Daragon that I've come to help him and that I know his friend Beorf! Please . . . please . . . I assure you, I mean no harm."

The young gorgon seemed sincere, but as a measure of precaution, Amos requested that she be blindfolded and that her hands be bound behind her back. Two of the knights who had escorted the visitor obeyed the order with caution. She was then taken close to the bonfire to be in full light. About twenty soldiers, their shields turned toward her, encircled Medusa. Now the gorgon could not flee without seeing her own reflection.

Surprised to have heard the girl pronounce Beorf's name, Amos approached her.

"I am Amos Daragon," he said. "You wanted to speak to me. Well, I'm listening."

"Yes," she answered. "I know Beorf. I turned him to stone myself. Don't judge me now; let me first tell you my story and you'll understand the circumstances that led to this unfortunate event."

Confounded by the news, Amos fell speechless. He felt guilty for having gone to the woods of Tarkasis without his friend. It was his fault that Beorf had been petrified. He had let him face a terrible danger alone, and now he was paying dearly for it. For an instant, Amos wanted to order the knights to kill the young gorgon. But he changed his mind.

"Go on," he told her as he sat on the ground. "I'm listening."

"The sorcerer you're about to fight is named Karmakas. He belongs to the race of humanimals, like your friend Beorf. He has the ability to morph into a snake, and thanks to his powerful magic, he can control all creatures related to reptiles. That is why the hairs of gorgons are his slaves. I must tell you that Karmakas sent me here to charm you before changing you into a statue. It's the same trap that your friend fell into.

"Beorf was captured by Karmakas and refused to tell him where the skull pendant was hidden. So I was told to free him to gain his trust. Afterward Beorf and I took refuge in a cavern that his parents used as a pantry, and we got to know each other. Beorf quickly fell in love with me. I was prudent because I knew that Karmakas was listening to our conversations to discover where the pendant was hidden and that he was waiting for the right moment to strike. When Beorf finally trusted me, he revealed the whereabouts of the pendant. That's when Karmakas came out of the shadows. He threatened to kill me unless Beorf brought him the pendant. Beorf obeyed, and when he came back, I turned him to stone.

"Only later did I realize how much I missed him. I couldn't stop thinking about him. I've gone back to the cavern every day since then, to see his frozen body. Now I know what friendship is . . . maybe even love. This kind of feeling does not usually exist among gorgons. So this has been a great revelation for me. I am truly sorry, and I came here to make amends for what I did. I'm willing to betray Karmakas and to tell you secrets that you'll be able to use against his powers."

Amos was touched by Medusa's account. He sighed and

kept silent a moment. "This won't bring back my friend," he said finally.

"You know, he talked a lot about you," the young gorgon answered. "I know that you don't get discouraged easily, and I know how to bring Beorf back to life. Win this battle, take back the city, and I'll give you your friend just as he was before."

"How can I trust you after what you just told me?" Amos asked. "Who says that this isn't a trick to help Karmakas?"

"Let me finish, then you'll decide if I'm loyal to you. I know the sorcerer's plans. He'll attack you as soon as you take the road to Bratel-la-Grande. He'll sense your presence and send hordes of venomous vipers against you. I know these animals well and it takes only one bite from them to send their victims into a deep coma. Their venom moves slowly to the heart and blocks all the arteries. Death is certain for whoever is bitten. I know also that Karmakas has a basilisk. I can't tell you what a basilisk is. I only heard him mention it a few days ago."

Amos frowned. "I was right, then. The pendant contained a rooster's egg. I know the power of this animal—the basilisk."

"Good, because Karmakas will not hesitate to use it against you. And that's not all. Inside the city walls, an army of gorgons is eager to wage battle. Karmakas's two hundred warriors are bored and squabble all the time to amuse themselves. They've pilfered the knights' weapons storehouse and have all kinds of swords, bows, spears, and clubs at their disposal. You and your men seem to know the secret to killing gorgons. I realized that as soon as I heard one of your men give the order to raise the mirrors. But I must tell you that this is also the only way to bring the city inhabitants back to life. The stone statues will be immediately freed of the curse when the gorgons who petrified them die as they see their own reflections. You know, I'm sorry that—"

Amos interrupted her. "If I understand properly, the only way to free Beorf from the curse is for you to look at your reflection in a mirror?"

Gravely, Medusa nodded. "I know how to free Beorf," she said. "Trust me. Let me help you by redeeming myself. I promise I'll give you your friend back. Consider me an ally. My help will be invaluable. I have a few good ideas to ensnare Karmakas. With my knowledge and your cleverness, we can defeat him."

## —17—

## THE BATTLE

Led by their lord Junos, the Knights of Equilibrium reached Bratel-la-Grande just before sunrise. The night had been long and sleepless for the men of Berrion. Heavy clouds hung in the sky. The pale light of dawn tarnished the landscape around the capital. The sinister atmosphere filled the knights with anxiety. Even Junos looked gloomy and he had lost any trace of his good humor.

From the top of the highest tower in the castle, Karmakas rejoiced when he saw the Berrion army take position in the fields. The sorcerer stroked the head of his basilisk tenderly. The creature had hatched the day before. Now, Karmakas put it down in a gold cage at his feet.

"Be patient, little one, *ssss*, my little treasure," he said with affection. "It will soon, *ssss*, be your turn to act."

The sorcerer raised his arm. He concentrated and repeated

a magic formula in an ancient dialect. In the fields, the knights saw a black cloud rise above the city.

"Stay on your horses and get ready to flee quickly," Junos shouted to his men. "If Amos is right, we'll easily win this first encounter."

Karmakas continued his incantation. A strong wind rose over Bratel-la-Grande and pushed the dark cloud toward the army. Suddenly, midway between the walls of the city and the spot where the Berrion men were, the cloud exploded in a deafening thunder. Hundreds of asps and cobras fell from the sky like a rain of swarming and slimy pieces of rope. The horses reared up and several knights were about to run off.

"*Keep your position! Keep your position!*" Junos shouted as he galloped in front of his men.

The army remained in place as the snakes crawled toward them upon touching the ground. They moved through the high grass in the fields like an ocean wave coming quickly to shore.

"*Prepare the cages!*" Junos ordered.

Every knight reached for the cage doors containing the starving mongooses. The snakes were arriving rapidly and were now only a few yards away from the horses. From the top of his perch, Karmakas looked at the sight with glee. He sniggered and rubbed his hands, sure that his snakes would quickly destroy these conceited humans.

"*Free the mongooses!*" Junos shouted when the time was right.

The doors of four hundred cages, containing one or two mongooses each, opened in unison. Seven hundred and seventy-seven small mammals that had been starved for days pounced onto the reptiles. The knights bolted away at full gallop. Being more agile than the snakes, the mongooses were jumping through the air, avoiding the fangs of their enemies and inflicting them with deadly wounds at each attack. As quick as lightning, their paws immobilized the cobras on the ground, while their strong teeth crushed the cobras' heads. The mongooses caught the asps by their tail and twirled them in the air. Dizzy, the small snakes lost their reflexes, which allowed the mongooses to pin them to the ground and inflict a deadly bite. Although superior in number, the reptiles were completely overwhelmed. There was no escape, no place to hide.

The battle lasted hardly ten minutes. About twenty mongooses lost their lives. Around the surviving ones, thousands of snakes lay lifeless in the grass. The mongooses began to feast under Karmakas's eyes.

The sorcerer seethed with rage. He stamped his feet, howling insults in his naga language and shaking his head in disbelief. How had the Berrion army known that he was going to send a cloud of snakes to rain over them? He had used this magic trick often, and few had ever managed to survive! As he looked at the unscathed men of Berrion, who were returning to their position in the fields, he smiled a tight smile.

"You've now, *ssss, met your end!*" he shouted.

Karmakas opened the cage of the basilisk and took the horrible creature in his hands.

"Go and shred, *ssss*, this band of buffoons!" Karmakas ordered it.

Amos and Medusa were hiding in the tall grass, not far from the walls of Bratel-la-Grande. From this strategic spot, the mask wearer could easily see the city gates through a telescope. He was happy with what the mongooses had accomplished and waited confidently for the rest to unfold. He knew that Karmakas would be enraged and would unleash his basilisk. Amos had his rooster on his knees and was ready for the next round.

He had evaluated the situation and sent his orders to Junos in a sphere of wind. Suddenly the gates of the city opened. The basilisk—the size of a large hen—came out. He was exactly as described in the book that Amos had read: His body was snakelike, but he had the head of a rooster and the beak of a vulture. He walked on two thin, featherless legs much like those of a chicken.

Amos and Medusa blocked their ears with a thick paste made of ferns. Then Amos uttered a few words that the wind carried away to Junos.

"*Stop your ears!*" Junos shouted to his men.

Wasting no time, all the knights blocked their ears with the fern paste. So far everything was going according to plan. Nothing had been left to chance. But when the basilisk took flight, Amos was stunned to see the creature's body grow tenfold. He then saw the basilisk open its beak. Right away Amos understood that the beast was shrieking out its paralyzing cry. Medusa grabbed the telescope from Amos and confirmed that the soldiers did not seem to have suffered. Only the horses were motionless.

Amos concentrated on creating a sphere of communication in his right hand. Then he raised his other hand and made the wind blow in the direction of the basilisk. The hideous bird-creature flapped its wings furiously to reach the knights. But the wind was too strong and the basilisk was hardly advancing. Amos had to maintain his focus to command the wind. He had trained a good deal before leaving Berrion, but this exercise always quickly drained him of energy. The intense attention it required gave him horrible headaches.

The basilisk kept making huge efforts to move forward, but Amos was putting a difficult obstacle in front of it. The mask wearer was sweating heavily. He had to wait for the right moment—for his rooster to crow—his right hand firmly holding the sphere of communication, his left hand still raised. He felt his legs weakening. The rooster was at his side, unconcerned. Amos was gradually losing his grip on the wind, and the basilisk was gaining ground. To delay the flying creature, Junos signaled for a volley of arrows to be unleashed. They rained down on the basilisk, causing the beast to falter slightly.

Karmakas gnashed his teeth, his lips foaming, as he looked upon the scene. He couldn't understand why the wind had picked up and how the knights were still able to move. A second volley of arrows took off. The basilisk was wounded in the thigh. Strangely enough, this seemed to increase its strength tenfold. It used all its energy to fight the wind and was getting closer to the Berrion army.

At last, Amos's rooster let out a loud *cock-a-doodle-doo*. Warned by Medusa, who had unblocked her ears, Amos turned around and imprisoned the animal's song in a sphere of wind. At that precise moment, he lost his focus and the wind stopped blowing. The basilisk surged headfirst toward the knights. His stare burned their hair and beards, as well as the manes and tails of the horses. Exhausted, Amos managed to launch his sphere in the basilisk's direction.

"Catch this, I have a message for you!" he shouted.

What followed brought two large tears of rage to Karmakas's eyes. The rooster's song, locked in the ball of air, reached the basilisk and filtered into its ears. It was the only one to hear the rooster's song—and it exploded in midflight, a few yards from Junos. Shouts of victory rose from the army of knights. They unblocked their ears and congratulated each other. There were a lot of handshakes and embraces. Amos had time to smile slightly before he passed out, drained by his efforts.

When Amos regained consciousness, Medusa was by his side. He had been taken to a temporary shelter and the young gorgon was watching over him.

"What happened? Where am I?" he asked.

"You're awake at last! You've been asleep for two days!" Medusa answered.

Amos sat up, totally horrified. *"Two days! I've been asleep for two days?"*

"Yes," the gorgon said. "But don't worry, the knights have everything under control—for now."

"Tell me what happened. Tell me everything."

"We took control of the situation," Medusa began. "After the basilisk died, Karmakas sent dozens of pythons and boas down the walls of Bratel-la-Grande. They were huge and strong, with bodies as thick as tree trunks. But the knights felt confident and were motivated by their two previous victories, so they attacked the snakes. It was a tough fight and several knights were wounded. But Junos shouted orders and himself killed at least a dozen of the beasts with his sword. Thanks to him, we won the battle. A while later, a slight earthquake shook the castle of Bratel-la-Grande. Nobody knows why or how this happened."

"But what's going on now?" Amos asked, alarmed.

"The knights worked tirelessly. They dug trenches, put up wood fences, lit fires that burn night and day, and patrol outside the city relentlessly. Their shield-mirrors are directed toward the city constantly, and the gorgons don't dare to look outside the walls. Karmakas is no doubt planning another attack against Junos and his men. The knights are very tired, and some fell asleep during their watch. It's impossible to take the city: its walls are too high. The gorgons send arrows on everything that moves. It would be suicidal to try to approach the city, and it isn't feasible to smash down the huge gates. Junos does not know what to do anymore. He's waiting impatiently for you to wake up and devise a new attack strategy."

"Very well," Amos said. "Unlike the knights, I am well rested. And I have a plan. Tell me where Junos is and let's finish this battle."

Ψ

Karmakas had gone back to his laboratory totally bewildered. For the first time in his life, he had lost three consecutive battles. It was unheard of for a sorcerer as powerful as he was. He felt ashamed and dishonored. In his rage, he hit the table in front of him with his fist. It took him a while to notice that the walls of the room had changed. Skulls, femurs, and tibias decorated his laboratory now. In an instant, he knew that Seth had left his world to come and talk to him. Slowly he turned around and saw his master's golden throne behind him. The snake-god, comfortably seated, was looking at him with scorn.

"How dare you treat me this way!" Seth bellowed as he crossed his legs. "I offer you a rooster's egg, and first you allow the egg to be stolen by the Knights of Light. Then, after years of searching for it, you recover my precious gift and you lose the hatched basilisk in the most miserable way. How can I continue to trust you and show you my goodwill?"

Karmakas lowered his head and begged for his master's mercy. "I am, *ssss*, sorry. I underestimated my, *ssss*, enemies. I thought that—"

"*You thought!*" Seth thundered, making the earth quake. "*A plague on you! Either win this war or I'll crush you, you stinking reptile! Now go and show me that you're worthy of my godly power and of my trust!"*

The whole castle shook and cracks appeared in the foundation. Then the walls of bones vanished into thin air, and Seth's temple disappeared, replaced by Karmakas's laboratory. The sorcerer fell to the ground, his head in his hands, trembling with anxiety and rage. After a few seconds, he tried to gather himself. He rushed to his book of magic and started to study some powerful spells. For a long time, he stayed locked in his laboratory.

ψ

While Amos and Junos were establishing a plan to take back the city, Medusa went in secret to visit Beorf. He was a pitiful sight. The young gorgon caressed his head tenderly.

"You'll soon be free, Beorf," she whispered in his ears. "I know that you can hear me. Your body is now of stone, but your soul is still here, hoping and waiting to be delivered. I've come to see you for the last time. You're the first and only friend I've ever had. I'll never see you again, but you'll be in my heart forever. Keep the sight of my eyes in your memory. You're the only person who's admired them. Thank you for your friendship and your kindness. Thank you for believing in me. I'll show you that I was worthy of your honesty and of your feelings. Good-bye, my friend."

Medusa kissed Beorf on the cheek and left the cavern, totally distressed by this final visit.

The gorgon returned to the camp as the knights were preparing to enter the city. Night was about to fall and the army had to act swiftly. No one had noticed Medusa's absence. She saw that the men of Berrion were not wearing their armor. In secret, they had made life-size figures from branches and mud, and had dispersed them around the city. These strange scarecrows were attired in the knights' armor, helmets, and boots. From a distance, they looked like real humans. Only their stillness seemed a little odd, but one would have to watch them for a long while to understand the trickery.

Leading his warriors, Amos headed for the tunnel through which he had followed Beorf. The knights proceeded after him in tight order, with a torch ready to be lit tucked into their belts, a sword in one hand and a shiny shield in the other. Every shield had been modified. Thanks to leather strips, the knights were now able to carry them on their backs, a little like a tortoise shell. The entire army managed to go through the tunnel unnoticed and crawled over the ground to hide inside the city walls.

"I'll go to the castle with Medusa now," Amos said to Junos. "She'll take me to the sorcerer. Wait till you hear from me. I'll tell you when to attack."

Solemnly, Junos shook his friend's hand.

"At your disposal, Mask Wearer! Good luck, Amos! I think that Crivannia would be happy with her choice if she could see the way you're leading this fight."

"Thank you, Junos." Amos smiled. "See you soon."

Medusa entered the castle with Amos by her side. He was wearing a bag over his head, and his hands were tied behind his back. The young gorgon was pulling him behind her with a rope. She pretended to limp and was using the ivory trident as a cane. She easily passed in front of the gorgons keeping guard and went before Karmakas.

"I've captured the mask wearer, master," she said. "I bring him to you in person."

Abruptly, the sorcerer asked, "Why did you not turn him to stone, *ssss*, as I asked, *ssss*, you to do?"

"His powers are huge, Father, and he is resistant to my magic," she answered, lowering her head.

Karmakas approached Amos and pulled the bag off his head. When he saw his face, he burst out laughing.

"This is who you, *ssss*, captured? This is a mere boy, *ssss*, who dares to stand up to me?" He shook his head. "Well, come here, *ssss*, and watch what is going, *ssss*, to happen to your army!"

Medusa stood aside while Karmakas pushed Amos toward a balcony at the top of the highest tower of the castle.

"Look at my power, *ssss*, and watch your men die!"

The sorcerer lifted his arms and muttered a magic formula. From the fields surrounding the city, a thick yellow and green smoke rose. All around, and for perhaps half a mile, an opaque cloud covered the land and part of the forest.

"Whoever breathes this, *ssss*, air will die poisoned, *ssss*. Your knights will not, *ssss*, resist for long."

"My men are indestructible, Karmakas," Amos answered calmly. "In fact, they're still standing!"

The mask wearer focused hard, and by his sheer will made the wind rise. It slowly pushed away the thick cloud, and the sorcerer could see that, in the distance, all the knights still remained standing. They had not budged. The poison had had no effect on them.

"Who are you, *ssss*, young human?" the sorcerer asked, trying to keep his composure. "Who sent you, *ssss*, and how can you counter the effects of, *ssss*, my magic?"

"I am Amos Daragon, your worst nightmare!" Amos answered with a ferocious smile.

"Very well, *ssss*, we'll see what your knights can do, *ssss*, against this!"

Karmakas asked Medusa to keep an eye on the prisoner and left the room. Then he ordered the gorgons to gather in front of the great city gates. Amos lost no time in creating a sphere and sent a message to Junos.

"I believe Karmakas is preparing an attack. Get ready!"

In the gray shadows of sunset, Junos could see the gorgons band together in front of the city gates. On his command, the knights moved forward noiselessly among the ruins of houses and streets filled with debris, and formed a semicircle around the snake-haired women. None were to escape. The men of Berrion were tired and tense, but they knew that if they won this battle, they would be able to sleep before heading home.

Karmakas forced his way through his gorgons. "Now, *ssss*, go and annihilate this, *ssss*, miserable army!" he ordered. "Open the portcullis!"

Before anyone had time to activate the mechanism to open the portcullis, Junos shouted, *"The torches!"*

Almost four hundred torches were lit at the same time. The gorgons cried out in surprise and Karmakas ordered them to attack the intruders. Walking backward, the knights advanced toward the female warriors. Shield-mirrors were attached to their backs, allowing them to raise their torches with their right hand to give light. In their left hands, the men of Berrion held small pocket mirrors that helped to guide them along. Junos was the only one unable to find his.

Dozens of gorgons saw their reflection and howled with pain. Their insides were torn apart before they turned to dust. Surrounded, the snake-haired women tried to flee and opened the portcullis. Fifty-some knights were waiting for them on the other side with gleaming shields. This final blow struck down a good number of gorgons. And around Karmakas, one gorgon after another fell. The knights kept closing in, ensuring that all the gorgons were doomed. Meanwhile, Karmakas transformed himself into a giant rattlesnake and slithered out. He made his way to the tower of the castle. Furious, he repeated incessantly, "I'm going to kill you, Mask Wearer! Death unto you!"

From the top of the tower, Amos and Medusa watched the collapse of the gorgons.

"Thank you, Medusa," Amos said. "You have helped to save hundreds of human lives. Now this town can be reborn."

"I must tell you something important, Amos," she answered. "There is only one way to bring our friend back to life. You know what I mean as well as I do."

"I know what you're going to say, Medusa, and I'll never force you to look at your reflection," Amos said as the young gorgon moved away from him. Her hands were shaking and her legs seemed unsteady. "There must be another way to give Beorf his life back. Together, we'll find it."

"I know what I'm saying, Amos. And I know also that you'd never force me to do something against my will. You'd never sacrifice me to save your friend. Even though we've spent only this short time together, we've grown attached to each other. And you, Beorf, and I would make an unbeatable team. But it is not possible. I understand that true friendship can mean sacrificing oneself to save someone else. This is what Beorf taught me when he looked at my eyes. He could easily have killed me with a blow of his paw and his powerful claws. But because he was my friend, he didn't do it. Even after my disloyalty, he remained true to himself, true to his feelings for me. With you, too, I've known friendship. This is a beautiful quality in humans. Now it's my turn to show some humanity. Tell Beorf that I will always remember him, even in my death."

Medusa then took Junos's small pocket mirror out of her bag. She had taken it from him before the battle. Amos leaped forward to stop the young gorgon. It was too late. She had seen her reflection.

"It's true, Beorf, I really do have beautiful eyes!" Medusa whispered before crumbling to dust.

At that moment, a rattlesnake appeared through the slightly opened door and rushed over to Amos. On impulse Amos grabbed his trident, barely avoiding the reptile's gigantic fangs. Again the snake attacked. Amos rolled to the ground on his side, freeing himself from the sorcerer.

Amos looked at his trident. "If you really can do extraordinary things, now is the time to prove it!" he said.

Amos threw his weapon with force at the snake. The trident penetrated the body of his enemy, but only slightly. A layer of scales protected Karmakas.

"Do you believe, *ssss*, that you can fight me with, *ssss*, that twig? I am going to swallow you in *one bite*!"

As Karmakas lunged, he suddenly grew faint. The trident, still implanted in his flesh, was now shining with a pale blue light. Karmakas threw up some salt water. Then Amos saw something fantastic happen. The trident was slowly driven into the snake's body. The floor of the room turned to liquid and the walls began to ooze. Cascades of water poured down from the ceiling. Two mermaids emerged from the sodden floor and grabbed hold of Karmakas. They wrapped him in a net of seaweed, totally oblivious to Amos, who stood by, not understanding what was happening. The mermaids pulled the big snake through the floor and vanished as quickly as they had appeared. The water evaporated. In the blink of an eye, the room took on its usual appearance. Except for a broken mirror on the floor.

# —18—

## BARTHELEMY, LORD OF BRATEL-LA-GRANDE

When Beorf opened his eyes, he felt as if he had been sleeping for years. He sat on the ground to recover. He was famished. He ate some nuts and tried to remember what had happened before he was turned to stone. At first his only thoughts were of the gorgon. He had dreamed that Medusa was caressing his face. Many times her enchanting voice had soothed him in his dreams. Beorf had totally lost any notion of time. Then an image of Karmakas popped into his mind. Also that of his friend Amos, who had gone off to accomplish his quest. All these memories swirled in his head. He decided to leave the cavern and started to walk aimlessly in the forest.

All the dwellers of Bratel-la-Grande—the Knights of Light, the peasants, and the shopkeepers—left the side of the road where they had been displayed as statues and began to walk toward the city. At the city gates, the men of Berrion gave them a warm welcome. Every gorgon had crumbled to dust; now the curse was only a bad memory.

A large meeting took place in the center of the ruined city.

"Dwellers of Bratel-la-Grande! I, Junos, lord of the Knights of Equilibrium and ruler of the kingdom of Berrion, declare this city free! We fought evil and delivered you from the gorgons. Now I offer to rebuild this city with you, in harmony and respect."

"Go away!" a man shouted in the crowd. "There is only one ruler here—me." It was Yaune the Purifier; he approached the dais. "No one will tell the Knights of Light what to do and how to do it," he said. "Leave immediately and let me rebuild our city the way we want it."

A murmur rose from the crowd. Junos raised his hand to ask for silence.

"Citizens of Bratel-la-Grande, it is because of your lord that all of you nearly lost your lives," Junos went on. "Yaune the Purifier knew that a powerful sorcerer was looking for him. He did not tell you the truth, and this lie almost brought your destruction. A true knight never tells falsehoods the way this man did for countless years. Today I must clearly state the facts so that all of you can understand my intentions. I ardently wish to annex Bratel-la-Grande's territory to that of Berrion's. Together we can create a vast kingdom—"

"How dare you!" Yaune shouted, drawing his sword. "I will not tolerate further insults."

Barthelemy jostled his way to the dais. "Yaune, should we

not listen to what this man has to offer? We owe him our lives, and were it not for his courage, this city would still be in the hands of our enemies. As proof of respect for the bravery of his men and to show my gratitude, I am ready to take an oath of allegiance to him. There is nothing wrong with serving someone who is stronger than oneself. When a lord who is good and fair requests an alliance, a knight must recognize his value and submit."

"*Traitor!*" Yaune cried loudly. "You speak like your father! And since we're putting all our cards on the table today, I'll confess that I'm the one who killed him with my own sword. We were together when the pendant fell into my hands. Your father insisted that we destroy it. I refused. That trophy was mine. He challenged me to a duel and I drew his blood. Now I order that you be burned alive for treason. Knights of Light, seize this man immediately!"

Baffled, the knights looked at one another. "We've burned enough innocent people!" one of them shouted. "I side with Barthelemy! Let his punishment be mine too, for I am tired of obeying Yaune the Purifier."

Another knight came to Barthelemy's side and put his hand on his shoulder. "I've known this man since childhood, and I believe he's got what it takes to become our new lord! I'm also in favor of an alliance with our saviors, our friends from Berrion."

The crowd applauded loudly and every Knight of Light gathered behind Barthelemy, their new master. Then Junos requested silence once more.

"Bratel-la-Grande has just chosen a new ruler!" he said. "Barthelemy, join me on the dais and listen to the acclamation of your people! Today I pledge to you the friendship and loyalty of Berrion. To facilitate our trade activities, we will build a road between our two kingdoms. We'll work together for the prosperity and well-being of our people."

Enraged, Yaune raised his sword to strike Barthelemy. Junos's guard stopped him.

"Let him be!" Bathelemy intervened. "For having killed my father, Yaune, I condemn you to exile. We will tattoo the word 'murderer' on your forehead so that everyone knows what kind of man you are. You will also be stripped of your title of knight. No one will be burned in this kingdom from here on. We will rebuild this city on new principles."

In the meantime, Amos looked for Beorf in the crowd. He did not find him, so he decided to leave the city and search beyond its walls. Luckily, a full moon helped him see clearly in the night. As he walked through the fields, Amos was relieved to see Beorf appear at the edge of the forest. He called to him and ran to greet him.

"Amos, my friend!" Beorf cried out as the two friends hugged each other. "How happy I am to see you again! I'm looking for Medusa. I want you to meet her, but she has disappeared. Yet she was with me when . . . It's the sorcerer who—"

"Beorf, we have many things to say to each other," Amos interrupted. "Let us sit down and let me tell you an incredible story of friendship."

Amos shared Medusa's feelings with Beorf. He also revealed that she had sacrificed herself for him. Beorf couldn't hold back his tears.

"I'll never see her again, then. Isn't that so, Amos?"

"I'm afraid that's true, Beorf."

A heavy silence fell upon them.

"She was so sweet and so beautiful," Beorf finally whispered. "I loved her. I spent the most wonderful moments of my life with her. And her eyes . . . You should have seen her eyes."

"I have to confess that I did my best to avoid seeing them," Amos said. "Come now! Let's go back to the city. We need distractions."

Along the way, Beorf remembered that the last time he had seen Amos was when Amos had left to go to the woods of Tarkasis.

"Tell me, Amos, do you know now what a mask wearer is?" Beorf asked.

"Oh! Indeed I do! Watch carefully."

Amos concentrated, slowly lifting one of his arms. A light breeze rose and surrounded the two friends.

Wearing an indelible mark on his forehead, Yaune the Purifier was locked in a wooden cage, carried away to the border, and exiled from the kingdom. Once released from his cage, the former ruler of Bratel-la-Grande took to the road like a beggar. The tattoo betrayed his true nature, and he was driven away from each village he crossed.

One night he unknowingly entered the realm of Omain,

ruled by Lord Edonf. There Yaune saw a small temple. He went inside, thinking that it would be a good spot to get some rest. A shiver went down his spine when he realized that the walls were made of human bones. Facing him, seated on a throne of gold, was a snake-headed creature. His skin was light red and his hands looked like strong eagle talons.

"Who are you and what are you doing here?" Yaune asked bravely.

"My name is Seth and I have a proposition for you. I offer you this sword, brave knight. It tears through armor and poisons all those it touches. A lord such as yourself cannot live without a kingdom. If you agree to be in my service, I'll provide you with power and wealth. Your mission is simple: conquer the land of Omain and kill the ruler, Lord Edonf."

"And if I refuse?" Yaune asked.

Seth smiled. "Well, if you don't accept my offer, you'll return to your life as a beggar and you'll die poor, famished, and forgotten. Conquer the realm of Omain and I'll offer you revenge over Barthelemy and Junos. You will recapture your former kingdom plus that of Berrion. Are you interested in my offer?"

Yaune smiled happily and extended his hand. "Give me the sword, Seth. I have a great deal of work ahead of me!" he answered.

# MYTHOLOGICAL LEXICON

## *The Gods*

**Lady in White:** A woman of legends and tales found in many different cultures, the Lady in White helps humans accomplish their destiny.

**Seth:** In Egyptian mythology, Seth is the god of darkness and evil. The Egyptians linked him to the desert and often represented him as a man with a monstrous head. He is also linked to crocodiles and animals of the desert.

## *Creatures of Legend*

**Basilisks:** In Europe, the Middle East, and some countries of North Africa, the basilisk was considered one of the most abominable creatures in the world. Since all those who were unlucky enough to see a basilisk perished, its true appearance is controversial. In 1544, in *Cosmographia Universalis*, the scientist Sebastian Munster described the basilisk as a wingless eight-legged creature. In the grand palace in Bangkok, Thailand, one can see a statue representing a basilisk.

**Fairies:** Fairies exist in many European cultures. Their size varies from country to country. Each fairy is usually associated with a specific type of flower. These creatures protect nature, and time does not seem to affect them.

**Gorgons:** Gorgons are creatures of Greek mythology. In legend, they lived in the dry and mountainous areas of Libya. They were most often depicted as three sisters: Stheno, Euryale, and Medusa. Medusa was the most famous of the three and the only one who was mortal. The hero Perseus beheaded her.

**Humanimals:** Humanimals are present in the culture of every country. The werewolf is one of the most famous of these creatures. Sometimes kind, sometimes menacing, humanimals are divided into races and species. The full moon often plays an important role in the transformation of a human into an animal.

**Mermaids:** The origin of these sea creatures is not well known. They have appeared in the tales and legends of many cultures since antiquity. They are usually represented as very beautiful fish-tailed women who charm navigators.

**Merriens:** In Ireland, half-human sea dwellers are called merriens. A distinction can be made between them and other sea creatures because they always wear a red-feathered bonnet. This magic hat helps them reach their dwellings deep in the ocean. Females are very beautiful. The sight of a merrien is perceived as the omen of a storm. Merriens sometimes come ashore disguised as little horned animals.

**Nagas:** Nagas are humanimals that transform themselves into snakes. Most nagas are linked with aquatic surroundings; those that live in the desert are called lamies. Nagas can reach a length of fifteen feet in their reptile form and live almost four hundred years. They can be found in the Sahara, in India, and in South Asia.

*Available Now!*

# Amos Daragon #2

## THE KEY OF BRAHA

Having survived his first mission as Mask Wearer, Amos finds himself in new danger. An encounter with a mysterious girl sends him to Braha, the City of the Dead, where souls await judgment. To get there, Amos must give up his own life. And when he reaches Braha, he finds a place overcrowded with spirits, because the gods have locked the doors that lead to paradise and to hell.

A special key is said to unlock the doors—if it can be found—and unbeknownst to Amos, many are relying on him to use his ingenuity and intelligence to locate that key and restore order, as Mask Wearers are known to do. But Amos knows that even if he finds the key, he might never return to the world of the living.